PALACE OF PLEASURE

SILVER WOOD EN BOOK THIRTEEN

azel Hunter

CHAPTER ONE

WE CAME BACK in time to save the world, not to die trapped in Pompeii.

Summer Lautner backed away from the window of the jail cell. The long dormant volcano inside Vesuvius had erupted, pouring millions of tons of its fiery heart into the sky. The fifteen-mile-high plume had just collapsed, and now raced down the mountain's slopes in an enormous, gray and black cloud of death. The surge made no sound, appearing only as a massive billow of smoke and ash. Yet Summer knew in a few moments the superheated tephra would entomb her and every living thing in the city. That included the two men she loved, two Templars she didn't trust, and a Fae woman who had already survived being buried alive in a diamond crypt for ten thousand years.

We are not dying today. Not while I still breathe.

Power surged through Summer as she turned from the horrifying sight, and held out her hands.

"Form a circle, now, *quickly.*"

Michael Charbon nodded to Elettra GemSage, who took his hand and Troy Atwater's. The men clasped the hands of Lemuel Bowers and Cyrus Shelton, the two Templars, who then moved to flank Summer. When she took their hands she channeled her power through everyone, completing the circle.

As the volcanic surge reached the city, the stone floor beneath their sandals shook and cracked.

Summer could feel bits of pumice pelting her face as it flew through the window. The inside of their cell suddenly became like an airless blast furnace. Closing her eyes, she cast the time-traveling spell.

"From this time we must flee, take this circle of travelers to Shaanxi, the day ninth, the month January, the year fifteen fifty-six A.D. So may it be."

The time portal opened above them just as the volcanic flow engulfed Pompeii's forum. But Summer kept her mind and power focused on the circle. The unbearable heat blistering her skin vanished, and a moment later she stood in cool, silent darkness.

Shelton's large, hard hand tightened on hers.

"Are we buried, then?" he asked. But his deep, gruff voice echoed slightly. She felt him shift. "In a cave?"

"Be still, Templar," Elettra said, and muttered something in an ancient tongue.

Tiny white stars showered over her petite, ordinary-looking body, and changed it into Elettra's true form, which was that of a towering, golden-haired goddess. As Shelton gaped the Fae woman conjured a dozen small, floating amber light orbs which illuminated their surroundings.

"You are not wrong, Brother," Bowers murmured. "It's a *yaodong*, I think, a cave that serves as a home."

Summer glanced around her. The cave-house seemed very tidy, with sparse furnishings that had been neatly made from wood. Along the edges of one wall stood a row of baskets and clay pots filled with uncooked rice and dried fruit. Herbs had been hung to dry from a long rope made of woven vine. Large straw hats stood stacked beside a heavy drape of patched, worn fabric. It all seemed appropriate for medieval China, but the air smelled dry and musty, as if the *yaodong* had remained empty for some time.

"Let's see if anyone else is here," Bowers said.

He gestured for Elettra to lead the way, followed by the bigger Templar. But neither Michael nor Troy joined them. Summer looked up to find Michael's jade-green eyes and sooty, muscular body glowing with one of Elettra's golden lights.

"Come here, Beauty," he said.

Summer hadn't realized how badly she was shaking until he pulled her against him and wrapped his strong arms around her.

"I'm sorry," she whispered. "That was too close."

"You kept us alive," Troy said, embracing them both. His vivid blue eyes looked deep into hers. Then he kissed her brow. "That's enough."

For a moment she allowed herself to take comfort from their embrace. Troy and Michael had been destined to become her sentinel mates, but since they had bonded they had become much more than that. Summer loved her men so much she could no longer imagine life without them. In times of great danger, she often had to act to protect them, but they were her partners as well as her guardians.

"I was careless," she said, holding on to both of them, "and we underestimated Wickerman. That can't happen again."

She needed to focus on their quest, as impossible as it seemed. All they needed to do was chase a murderous rogue warlock through time, and find four hidden Fae crystals before he destroyed the world with them. She let go a heavy sigh and rested her face against Michael's warm chest. Wickerman had already stolen RainLance, the crystal of water concealed in the tip of a spear. It had been lost along with Pompeii. But she also felt convinced that the killer and his cultists had somehow caused Vesuvius to erupt prematurely.

"What is done is done," Michael said, his deep voice rumbling in his chest. "It does no good to dwell on it."

Summer slowly nodded. Through the telepathic link that she, Troy, and Michael shared, he had heard her thoughts.

"We're in sixteenth-century China now," Troy said, his gentle voice just behind her ear. "The cultists left just before we did. We stand a fighting chance of finding TerraCairn before they do."

The crystal of earth would be swallowed up in the worst earthquake in human history. But if Wickerman managed to find it first, and moved through time to collect the other two, there would be no future for any of them.

"There is no one here," Elettra announced.

As the room brightened, Summer reluctantly separated from her men. She turned to watch Bowers and Shelton pull aside a drape and look out of a long, brick-lined opening. Beyond it were other buildings.

"We cannot leave," Michael said, and tugged at his own tunic. "We are still dressed like Romans, and our satchels are now buried with Pompeii."

Elettra peered outside. "I see no one out there. I will go and find proper clothing for us."

Another shower of stars changed her back into her mortal guise. Before anyone could speak she walked outside. Shelton gave Summer a pointed look before he followed after the Fae.

"I have some knowledge of China in this era," Bowers said, as he moved to the back of the room. "The people live in caves they excavate out of the loess cliffs. They are not made of stone, but a wind-blown silt that has accumulated over the centuries. It's why so many are going to die in the Great Shaanxi Earthquake." He reached out and raked his hand down the wall, sending bits of yellow gravel and dust raining down. "Loess is little more than hard-packed dirt."

"How many will die?" Michael asked.

The short, fair-haired Templar exchanged an unhappy look with Michael.

"Our records indicate only an estimate. But the quake will destroy more than five hundred square miles, and kill over half the population."

"How many is that?" Summer asked.

Bowers grimaced. "Over eight hundred thousand souls."

• • • • •

Elettra stopped in the center of the dust-caked wooden bridge to survey the deserted village. She had not seen a single mortal since leaving the cave-house, and it seemed all the other dwellings had been abandoned. At first the empty pens made sense. People leaving a place always took their livestock with them. But then she saw the wide swaths of rusty stains curdling the soil. Small twig cages that hung from poles swung in the cold, dry wind. Some still held the dead, shriveled remains of song birds left to starve.

She paused at a well cover, and brushed away a thick yellow layer of silt. Lifting it away revealed a rope tied to its underside. Several hand-over-hand pulls brought up some water in a bucket. Though it was drinkable, she wiped her mouth on the back of her hand. Even the water tasted like tears.

Dry leaves scuttled across the discolored ground. The hollow moan of the wind might have come from her own heart. Had they somehow brought death with them from Pompeii? The grit of ash still lingered on Elettra's skin. She had felt a queer kind of relief when she saw the volcano's spew rushing toward them. It had promised to release her from more than her long life. She hadn't known Summer could cast the time-jumping spell so quickly. But she had, and now Elettra would have to live on, and betray her Wiccan friends. If she didn't steal the crystals once they had been recovered, and kill the two Templars, the Fae king had promised to bury her alive again—this time for eternity.

"A penny for your thoughts, lady," a deep voice said.

"I am not a lady, Shelton." She did not look at the big, dark Templar who joined her. Every time she did she wanted to punch him again. "Keep your penny and go away."

"They butchered the stock," he said, "but took the people." He nodded toward the dirt road leading away from the village across the plateau. "You can still see where they were marched out."

"They did not go slowly, or willingly," she said.

Shelton gave her a questioning look. She nodded at the twig cages. "They would have freed their birds before they left."

Feeling tired now, she walked across the bridge to the nearest cave-house, and ducked inside to search for suitable clothing. When she emerged Shelton took the bundle of what she'd found and tapped a long, dirt-stained scroll pinned to one of the outer coverings.

"I've seen these all over the village," he said. "Bowers can read these marks, I think." He removed it and rolled it up.

"These people are small and thin," she said. "You and Charbon will have to wear cloaks over your Roman garments."

As she brushed past him Shelton caught her arm. "Why do you still disguise yourself as a Wiccan? We know that you are Fae."

Elettra looked down at his hand. "Do you wish to fight me again? I would be happy to beat you into the ground this time."

The reminder of their duel made him scowl, and he released her. His dark eyes searched her face as if seeking some flaw.

"No," he said. "I only wish to…never mind."

He turned and strode back toward the cave-house where the others waited.

Elettra felt a tingling where Shelton had touched her, and an ache where he had not. Everything about the wretched warrior-priest annoyed her. He had no magic or powers, but his every look seemed to bespell her. Long ago she had resigned herself to her lot. As the last surviving GemSage, and the traitor who had destroyed her own clan, she had made herself a pariah. No Fae clan would welcome her into their stronghold, and she would never find a mate among her own kind. The rest of her life would be spent in some solitary place, where she would look after herself, sculpt crystal again, and perhaps find some peace.

Shelton made her wish for more. Shelton made her want it. But he could give her naught but more wanting. She harrumphed before resuming her search in a different house. They would need proper footwear.

As she peered under some sturdy benches, footsteps approached from outside: not heavy enough to be Charbon or Shelton, not light enough for Bowers or Summer.

Atwater's shadow fell through the doorway.

"I thought I'd give you a hand," he said.

"I have two," she said, not turning. "That is plenty."

But when he didn't leave, she stood.

"Why did Vesuvius erupt too early?" he asked.

If Atwater knew just how malevolent the four crystals her clan had created were, he might not ever feel safe near them or her again. She shrugged.

"Perhaps it was because Charbon stopped a horse from trampling his handler. Or perhaps it was because the sea became like lead when Wickerman's minions stole RainLance from the Temple of Neptune. Our breath in the air, our steps on the ground, the food we ate, the people we spoke to—none of it should have happened, but it did, and it changed the past."

The dark warlock started to say something, and then looked puzzled.

"The pressure did change while we were fighting underwater," he said.

Elettra retrieved some woven straw sandals and a pair of wooden clogs from under the bench.

"RainLance did not wish to be taken," she said. "I wager it made the sea heavier to hurt us."

"Gods," Troy muttered and dragged a hand over the back of his neck. "That has to be why the mountain blew too early. The increased pressure from the heavier water."

"How can that be?" Elettra said. "The

11

mountain was miles from the shore. The water never touched it."

"We're seeing the same thing in our time," he said. "As the glaciers melt, the sea level rises and increases the pressure on the earth's crust, which in turn results in more volcanic activity. By doing the same thing much more rapidly, RainLance triggered a premature eruption." He paused and studied her face. "Do you think it was trying to kill us?"

"I cannot say," she said, keeping her face as bland as her tone. She handed him some of the footwear as she headed to the door. "We have enough shoes."

They walked back to the cave-house together, where Summer was lighting some simple oil lamps. Elettra and Troy handed out the shoes while Bowers sat at a low table examining the scroll Shelton had found. He had already changed into a padded indigo jacket and some faded hemp trousers.

"Can you read their odd little picture writing?" Elettra asked him.

"The *hànzi* are primitive," the Templar said. "But I can still make it out." He glanced up at Summer and her mates. "This was a decree issued by the governor of the province. If my translation is correct, then I'm afraid it's rather grim news. At least for the villagers."

Troy pulled off his tunic and shrugged into a wide-sleeved brown overshirt.

"Read it to us," he said, as Charbon and Shelton slung large capes over their broad shoulders.

Bowers stretched out the scroll. "It says: 'If any under rule of Chang Xishan, the venerable and esteemed Shaanxi governor, do congregate unlawfully, create disturbances, transgress the laws or excite rebellion, they shall be punished for their crimes under the statutes of the empire direct. This decree is given that all of the people of Dingcuan village are guilty of such crimes, and shall serve in the governor's mines until he is stirred to forgiveness. Oppose not the mighty Xishan's decree, or submit to slow slicing.'"

"Slow slicing of what?" Summer asked, looking perplexed.

"The body," Bowers said, his voice bleak. "The practice is known in our time as *lingchi*. They tie the prisoner naked to a pole in a public place, and go to work very slowly with a blade. They slice away at the condemned until he dies, or a thousand cuts have been made. To add to their suffering some prisoners are kept alive for days, even weeks." He looked up at Summer. "The entire village left to work as slaves in the governor's mines so they wouldn't be cut to death."

CHAPTER TWO

ONCE THEY HAD changed into the native clothing, Summer gathered everyone around a work table. When the team had been formed, centuries of Templar records had weighted heavily in favor of Bowers and Shelton being included. It was time for them to put some of their specialized knowledge to work.

"Where do you think TerraCairn was hidden?" she asked.

Bowers laid a plain cloth over the table. Using a piece of charcoal from the *yaodong's* hearth, he sketched a crude map.

"This is where we are," he said, drawing an x, "and this is the plateau." He drew a roughly oblong outline around it. Outside the outline he created a black dot. "This is Huaxian." He drew a wavy line between the plateau and the black dot.

"A Portuguese trader saw Kember get off a river boat and enter the city," he said, referring to the Fae warrior who had originally traveled back in time to hide the four treasures for the king. "He came in carrying sacks of gems, and he didn't bother to disguise himself." Bowers crossed his arms over his chest. "At the time foreigners were still welcome in China. Unfortunately for us, the Ming dynasty of this era are isolationists." He gazed around at each of their faces. "They have since outlawed foreign trade."

"We don't plan to pose as traders," Summer told him. "We can just be travelers from the south heading for Russia. We can say it's our homeland."

"That's not going to work very well under the new regime's laws," the Templar said.

"In a few years from now Jesuits will arrive to serve the Ming court as astronomers and map-makers," Shelton said. "That can be our cover for this time. If we come into the city from the north road, we can even say that the Jiajing emperor sent us to survey the area." As everyone stared at him he shrugged. "I knew some mortals who belonged to the Society of Jesus. They were all clever and kind men."

Michael eyed him. "The Jesuit order had no female branch."

"But they don't know that," Troy countered. "As imperial map-makers we can go anywhere."

"Then it's decided," Summer said. "Thank you, Mr. Shelton."

Knowing they'd need to stop and eat along the way, Summer gathered the food that was still edible and piled it in a basket. The villagers had sun-dried apple and pear slices, and made raisins from grapes. She even found some blocks of dried curd, and sealed pots of root vegetables pickled in rice vinegar. Elettra brought a large bag of nuts and two bulging hide water containers to add to their stores.

"We will be able to buy food in the city," the Fae woman said, and handed Troy a small, heavy cloth pouch. "I found it hidden in the largest cave-house."

He opened it and poured a handful of rough, dark-green jade nuggets onto his palm.

"No doubt we will," he said. "What a hoard."

Stepping outside made Summer appreciate the heavy robe and skirt that Elettra had found for her to wear. Even at mid-day the buffeting of the plateau winds chilled her fingers. She tucked her hands inside the voluminous sleeves, and set the broad straw peasant's hat to shade her eyes from the strong sunlight.

"Thanks to our translation spell tattoos we'll all be able to communicate with the locals," Bowers said. "But since I'm most familiar with these people and their history, once we reach Huaxian it would be best if I speak for the group." He smiled at Summer. "With your permission, of course, Ms. Lautner."

Michael replied before she could. "We can speak for ourselves, Templar."

Summer saw the two men tense as if to square off. Some of the reason for Michael's hostility came from the fact that the Templars had stolen him as an infant from his Wiccan family and raised him to serve the order. Only after they'd returned from an arduous adventure in Canada had her mate finally shed the last of his Templar ways—but he still carried a grudge. He'd also disliked Bowers from the moment they'd met, and she wasn't sure why. While the man was a Templar, he'd gone out of his way to be pleasant to everyone on the team.

"You can natter on about this all day," Shelton said, his tone sharp. "But if we wish to reach the city before dusk, do it while we're walking."

Bowers glared at his comrade, but Michael's fists loosened and he nodded.

"So Shelton is a peacemaker," Troy murmured

to Summer. "Interesting. Perhaps we should have *him* speak for us."

Silence fell over the team as they began the long, cold walk to Huaxian. Summer felt grateful for the chance to think. Losing RainLance to Wickerman in Pompeii had left them all stunned and angry. If they were to prevail over him and his cultists in this time, they had to do better. They could no longer assume anyone they met was genuine. The rogue warlock had fooled them all by posing as Floronius, their innkeeper. His ruse had allowed him to spy on them nearly the entire time they'd spent in Pompeii. He'd probably even had them followed whenever they'd left the inn.

She would have sworn that Floronius was nothing more than a bad-tempered, tightfisted native. Perhaps that was part of Wickerman's ability—to assume any identity. And what had happened to the real innkeeper?

He murdered the Roman, a grouchy voice said inside her mind. *Just as he has every mortal and immortal necessary to his purpose.*

The Emerald Tablet shared Summer's soul, and it could read her thoughts whenever it liked. It could be annoying, but this time she could use the entity's input.

Yes, but how does he take on their personality as well as their appearance?

The rogue can make living beings out of straw, Daughter, but to impersonate another requires old magic.

Elettra, who was walking beside her, gave her a strange look.

"Your eyes look like emeralds in the sun," the Fae woman said. "Emeralds that are on fire."

Summer forced a smile. "They change color sometimes."

The Fae woman chuckled. "They do not."

'Tis that old book inside you. When I am close to you, I can also hear it in my thoughts. It sounds like my grandmother did whenever she felt vexed, which was nearly always. Does it always feel vexed with you?

I imagine it does. Since she and Elettra also shared a telepathic link the revelation didn't startle Summer, but the Fae's understanding of the entity rattled her a little. *Remember, you must not say anything to the Templars about the Emerald Tablet. They cannot learn that I am its Guardian.*

If they do, I will turn them into frogs, and we will eat them. The Fae woman gave her an exaggerated wink. *I but jest, Summer. I hate frog. Antelope would be better.*

They stopped halfway to Huaxian to rest and eat, and then Troy walked with Summer to a spot that overlooked the valley. Below them a dozen roads wound along the terraced slopes to converge at a large city surrounded by high, thick stone walls. Within the walls lay hundreds of curved, stacked roofs made of light blue tiles. Each seemed to have been built to echo a much larger palace in the very center. Four black and red towers soared up into the sky at the compass points of the palace's compound, which appeared to take up a third of the city's entire area. Every roof inside the massive stronghold gleamed light gold, and hemmed dozens of courtyards filled with trees, gardens and glittering pools.

"Kember hid TerraCairn inside that place," Elettra said as she came to stand beside Troy. "I feel it now."

Troy glanced at her. "Can you tell exactly where it is?"

The Fae woman shook her head. "Once I am inside the walls, it will call to me, and I will track it from there."

Bowers intercepted them before they walked back.

"There's something you should know before we reach Huaxian," he said and pointed at the towered stronghold. "That is an imperial-class palace."

21

Troy's dark brows arched. "We didn't think it was a theme park."

"You don't understand," the Templar said, eying the city. "Yellow is an imperial color, reserved in this era for the exclusive use of the Ming emperor. If we were in Peking, the yellow roof tiles would make sense. Here, they do not—and before you ask, that is not Peking down there. The four towers of the Shaanxi governor's palace are very distinctive."

"Then why have they used the royal color here?" Elettra asked.

"Either the entire court moved to Huaxian," Bowers said, "Or someone who fancies himself an emperor built it."

• • • • •

Near sunset Michael took point as they fell in behind a group of porters trudging up from the docks of the river to the city gates. The fierce-looking guards allowed the porters to pass, but drew their swords and blocked Michael's path.

"Who are you?" one of them demanded.

"We are emissaries from the imperial court," Michael said. "Sent to survey the city." He felt Troy press the pouch of jade into his hand, and moved his arms behind his back as he extracted a few pieces. "May we show gratitude to those who guard Huaxian so well?"

The guard looked around before making a beckoning gesture. As Michael bowed, he discreetly handed over the jade. The guard quickly pocketed the bribe and smirked at his partner before he stepped out of the way.

Once inside Huaxian they walked down the paved streets among the locals, all of whom moved quickly and in silence with their eyes downcast. Despite seeing dozens of people Michael sensed emptiness all around them, as if they walked through a city of ghosts.

"We need rooms for the night," he said to Troy, who nodded.

"Excuse me," Summer said to a woman walking toward her. "Can you tell us where we might find—" She stopped as the woman darted around them and hurried away. "Or not."

"Allow me," Bowers said, and bowed to an older man standing in a doorway. "Honorable sir, would you be so kind as to—" As the Templar straightened, the man retreated and slammed the door shut. "Right."

They continued on and attempted to speak to anyone who crossed their path, with the same results. The people of the city didn't talk to them or each other, and behaved as if they were too busy. But their frantic pace didn't entirely conceal the terror they felt whenever Summer or someone else spoke to them.

"Is there some decree against speaking in this time?" Summer asked Bowers.

"Not in any of the histories I've studied," the Templar said. He strode up to a guard standing at the entrance to a large, red-walled building. "We have come from Peking," he told the man. "By order of the emperor, who wishes us to—"

The guard drew his sword and brought the edge up to press under Bowers' chin.

Summer summoned her power, and felt Troy and Michael do the same. But before they could move against the threat, a small, precisely-dressed man appeared and stepped between them and the guard.

"Peace at night, Watchman," the man said in a high-pitched voice. He covered his fist with his other hand and bowed to the guard. "I ask your forgiveness for this one's ignorance. I am Meng, master jeweler of the Lotus Quarter, sent to meet these emissaries. A cart overturned and blocked the street." He bowed again, making the wide silken sleeves of his immaculate brown tunic flutter like wings. "If you will permit, I will now take charge of them for the Master of All That is Our Joy."

Slowly the guard lowered his curved blade and flared his nostrils at the small man.

"You honor me with your merciful understanding, Watchman," Meng said, bowing so low his brow nearly touched his knees.

He backed away, and made a gesture for Michael and the rest of the team to follow him.

Summer didn't move, and Michael could feel her suspicion. Then he understood. How could Meng have known about their cover story? They'd told only the guards at the city gates. Was their rescuer in fact Wickerman, wearing yet another disguise? Had he killed the real Meng to take his place?

The watchman made an ugly sound in his throat, and Meng regarded Summer with visible impatience.

"Come quickly now," he said, "and do not speak."

Summer glanced at Bowers, whose neck sported a bloody gash, and reluctantly nodded to Michael.

Meng led them to a large house with black roof tiles and red-painted walls, ushering them inside before closing the sliding entry door and securing it with a row of locking latches. As they waited in the front hall he went around to close the shutters on the windows overlooking the street.

"Perhaps I missed something in the histories," Bowers said quietly, and gingerly wiped the trickle of blood from his neck.

Meng returned with a lamp, which he handed to Bowers.

"That was exceptionally foolish, Emissary," he told him. "The city's watchmen do not speak to strangers."

"Is that also true of the people here?" Michael asked. "We wished only to find an inn for the night."

"There are no inns open to outsiders," the jeweler said, "and idle talk within the city walls is forbidden. Now come to my tea room, and we will speak with purpose."

The interior of Meng's house proved to be as meticulous and tidy as his appearance, with fine silk tapestries displayed on the walls, and abundant, colorful hanging lanterns to illuminate the rooms. They crossed a square room that had no roof, and through the overhead opening Michael saw the deep violet sky beginning to spangle with thousands of stars.

"The Chinese do love their courtyards and sky wells," Bowers said, keeping his voice low. "There will be a shrine for the man's deities and ancestors in the center of the house. It is a sacred place of ceremony, so we must not trespass there."

Through an open door Michael saw a tidy work room that contained only three walls, a long stone-topped table, and a wooden stool. Delicate-looking tools had been placed in precise order on a cloth-covered tray beside a number of tiny wood and putty assemblages.

"I keep no jewels in the house at night," Meng told him, his expression impassive. "All of my work is stored in the palace treasure room until dawn, when I go to work there."

"We are not thieves, Master Meng," Michael said, ducking as they entered a small room with a low table surrounded by silk pillows. "We are map-makers, come to survey Huaxian for the emperor."

"This you say," the jeweler said. "This I believe." He bowed over his clasped fist. "Come and find comfort at my table."

Meng gestured for them to sit on the pillows, and clapped his hands three times. An older woman trotted in and bowed to him, remaining low.

"The best tea and food for my guests," he ordered.

Without a word the servant backed out of the room and vanished. Meng folded away some paper screens behind the table to reveal a long, wide opening to a garden of small trees and moss-splotched sculptures.

"I am shamed by how you were treated on your arrival," the jeweler said as he sat down at the end of the table. "In my youth we welcomed travelers, as they brought many fine things from the world beyond our borders. Indeed it is still my custom to frequent the city gates at dusk in hopes of such encounters." He frowned as he considered the floor. "Since the Ming have come to power, such courtesies have been severely curtailed."

"How did you know we were emissaries sent by the emperor?" Summer asked, drawing sharp looks from everyone.

"That is what your man told the guards at the gates," Meng said. "I was on the other side when you arrived." He regarded Michael. "Forgive me, but I think you do not come from Peking."

Troy gave Michael a warning look.

"Why do you say that, Master Meng?" the big man asked.

"I have travelled there many times," Meng said.

He offered them a polite smile. "Snow blocks the northern roads until the thaw, which has not yet come."

"We used the river," Michael said quickly.

"Ah, but then there are these two women with you, who do not behave like servants." Meng nodded at Summer. "That one's eyes and fruitful shape would catch the eye of the Jiajing at once. How does she yet not wear the yoke of royal concubine? Did you hide her from him?"

"We were not brought before your ruler, so that we might avoid such attention," Elettra said, startling him. "Nor are we serving wenches. She is wife, and I see to the comfort of all. Need you know more?"

Meng's cheeks pinked. "Forgive my assumption. I have not encountered many females from beyond the borders. I know well only one lady, in fact, and she is…well-protected." He shifted his gaze to Summer. "Lady, you should take care while you are here. There are men who would happily kill your husband and all your friends to take you as bed slave."

Michael folded his hands to emphasize the muscles of his arms and chest. "They may try."

"However you came, why would you willingly enter the city for any reason? Have you not heard the tales of our governor, the mighty Xishan?" Before anyone could answer the jeweler sighed. "Of course you have not. He will have seen to that. No one dares to speak of him or our troubles, for fear they will be next to suffer."

"We noticed that an imperial roof protects his palace," Bowers said. "That seems a dangerous defiance of the law."

"When the palace was built the roofs were of white tile, meant to reflect the sun during the hot months. One morning the city woke to find it newly-tiled in yellow. It frightened the people, for such work could not have been done by a hundred men over a moon cycle. Xishan saw to it in a single night." The jeweler hesitated, pressing his lips together as his shoulders sagged. "Huaxian has become plagued by strange magics, much of them unseen and unknown. Our city is bewitched now, and we live like hobbled mice among pregnant cats."

"We know your governor sent an entire village to his mines for insurrection," Troy said carefully.

"Ah, Dingcuan. Yes, they were foolish to let their talk of unfair taxes spread to the city." The jeweler patted his hair with three careful motions. "Xishan tolerates no opposition to his rule. We all of us could be sent to the mines for how we speak now."

The servant returned with a heavily-loaded tray, which she placed before Meng. He in turned poured the tea into tiny cups, which she served to Michael and the others along with small plates of artfully-decorated rice cakes, sliced sand pear and squares of speckled yellow curd.

Michael tasted the tea, which was strong and slightly bitter. "I understand that the people are not permitted to talk idly, but those we saw appeared very frightened as well."

"So they should be," Meng said, "outside so close to sunset." He dropped one of the curd squares into his tea cup. "When darkness falls, the streets of the city are patrolled by the governor's tigers. They will maul anything that moves, and they cannot be killed."

"Are they part of this strange magic you spoke of?" Bowers asked. "That could be why they seem invincible."

"You cannot kill what does not live, Emissary," the jeweler said. "The tigers that walk our streets are made of stone."

CHAPTER THREE

MENG SHOWED THEM to the guest rooms on the second level of his home, and directed his servant to provide them with fresh clothing and hot water for washing.

"There is a bath house by the stone garden," the jeweler told Bowers, nodding down the corridor back to the stairs. "But I find the meltwater from the mountains too cold to use in winter." He cast an eye over the group. "I will seek my bed now. Sleep soundly."

Bowers and Shelton bid them good-night before they retreated to their room, but Elettra lingered. As Summer, Michael, and Troy entered their room, she followed them inside. She inspected the tidy quarters and the richly-carved wooden cabinet that enclosed the bed on all but one side.

"Will all of you fit inside this?" she asked. "It seems very cramped."

"We'll manage," Summer said, as she closed the door and turned to her. She lowered her voice. "What did you think of Meng's story about the stone tigers?"

"TerraCairn was likely used to create them," the Fae woman said lowly. "Its power over the earth allows it to shape and animate such creatures. My clan planned to use it to build an army of stone warriors. Soldiers that could not be killed would defeat any clan, and protect their rule forever."

"So you think someone here has found the treasure, and is using the crystal?" Michael whispered. When Elettra nodded he glanced through the window grate at the palace. "It must be this cruel governor."

"There is something more I must tell you," Elettra said quietly. "Since we came into the city I have felt TerraCairn's power. 'Tis in every brick, stone, wall and street. I can sense no direction or source to track. Something has made it become part of the city itself."

"Or it's making you think that," Troy suggested. "In order to conceal itself."

"No, Atwater. As the last of the GemSage I am immune to crystal power. Naught but diamond can cloud my mind or confuse my senses." Elettra regarded Summer. "I think there is a powerful magician at work for this governor, one who uses TerraCairn. With the proper spell, he could make it seem as if it were everywhere and nowhere."

"Could Kember have sired another child while he was here?" Summer asked, thinking of the half-Fae brothel owner in Pompeii who had died trying to protect RainLance from Wickerman's cultists.

"I think not. It would feel different on my skin. So would Wiccan magic. This spell caster must be a Chinese who knows the secret of attaining immortality, like the Templars." Elettra smothered a loud yawn and went to the door. "I bid you good-night."

"We need to talk someplace where the walls aren't as thin as rice crackers," Summer said quietly, as she closed the door. She removed her jacket and made a face as a small shower of dust fell from it to the floor. "And I don't think one basin of water will wash the three of us."

"That's where I come in handy," Troy said, mischief twinkling in his vivid blue eyes. "Let's go down and have a look at Meng's bath house."

They retraced their path from the guest quarters to the tea room, and slipped out into the serene rock garden. A small tiled path wound around the mossy stones to a set of white steps leading into a miniature house. It had been fashioned from black and white painted wood, set with baked clay panels etched with flower and animal shapes. Inside a row of empty wood buckets sat on a slatted floor, waiting to be filled from reed spouts on the wall. On a shelf above the buckets lay cloths, brushes, and bowls filled with dried plants and flowers, rendered white fat, fine quartz sand, and grayish salt granules. Several clean robes had been left neatly folded on a bench.

The next room contained a large, shallow stone pool of clear water half-covered by ice. Beneath the water she could see curved stone perches and ridged brick footrests. More bowls of herbs and roots surrounded the edge of the soaking tub.

"Asians consider bathing to be medicinal as well as hygienic," Summer told her mates. "I know you're supposed to wash before you get in the tub. My guess is that you scrub yourself down with wet sand to remove dirt, rinse, and then repeat the process with sea salt to clean away any lingering odors. A third herbal scrub from head to toe, final rinse, and you're ready for a soak."

Summer found the chains which opened the

spouts, and filled three of the buckets as she inspected the bowls. "Chrysanthemum petals, dried ginger, crushed eucalyptus, and sea salt." She wrinkled her nose as she sniffed the bowl of fat. "And oh my. Rancid lard."

"Meng said he was not using the bath house," Michael reminded her.

"There's a bucket of wood ash over here," Troy said as he investigated the other side of the room. "Lye from soaked ashes plus lard makes soap."

"I think we'll stick to the sand, salt and herbs," she said. She nodded at the brimming buckets. "Help me warm those, please."

Troy spread his hand, and three spikes of his elemental power flashed blue over the cold water, heating it until wisps of steam danced from the buckets.

"If you want to talk," Troy said, "now might be the time."

"We cannot think when you are naked and wet," Michael said. He came up behind her, slid off her jacket, and stroked his palms over her shoulders. "Meng troubles you."

"He rescued Bowers from the watchman, and then brings us into his house, and treats us like family—all after just overhearing our story at the gates. He knows we didn't come from Peking, yet he completely accepts our story, and tells us tantalizing tales of strange magic and stone tigers." She leaned back against the hard vault of her golden warrior's chest. "I think Meng was sent to collect us, either by Wickerman, or whoever has TerraCairn."

"He does work for the governor," Troy said as he reached around her waist to untie her skirt. "And, if his story is true, Xishan replaced the roof of the palace in one night. That sounds like Fae magic to me. Perhaps Xishan is using TerraCairn to do such things."

"Or he might have painted the white tiles yellow," Michael said, and grinned as they both stared at him. "Not everything is done by great magic. Sometimes all you need is darkness, and a good trick."

Summer nodded. "We can assume nothing," she said and stepped out of her skirt. She lifted her arms so the big man could tug her linen shift over her head. "I want to try to send another message to Southbrook in the future. He may have made some progress on discovering who planted the bomb in our things before we left Boston." She went still and pressed her hand to her forehead. "And the messaging mirror is back in Pompeii with the rest of our gear."

"Whatever the head of the Magus Corps council has dug up won't be much help to us in this time anyway," Troy said as he stripped out of his clothes. He picked up a dipper and scooped up some of the steaming wash water. "Close your eyes."

Summer obeyed, and then sighed as he poured the water over her head.

"Oh, that feels amazing," she said but then gasped as a cascade showered over her and both men. *Troy.*

"If we use the dipper, washing will take all night." His eyes glittered with amusement and desire as he rubbed handfuls of the clean sand over his arms and chest. Then he pulled her against him and rubbed his chest and belly against hers. "Paladin, attend to her back side."

"My pleasure," the big man said.

He massaged the wet sand over her shoulders, down her spine, and over the curves of her bottom. Once she was coated from chin to ankles with the damp sand, her men pressed her between them, their fingers gently scouring her skin with their caresses.

"I feel like I've been rolling around on the beach with you two," she said, and shivered as the cold night air wafted in. "Can we rinse off now?"

Troy obliged by dousing them with the contents of another bucket, which sent the scrubbing sand streaming down their legs to disappear into the floor slats.

"Be gentle with the salt," Michael warned his sentinel brother as he took a handful from the bowl. "Crush it between your palms, or it will scratch her skin."

"I have a better idea," the dark warlock said. He brought the third bucket over, and added the sea salt to the water. Once Michael had done the same he drew the cloudy water up to hover like a dense cloud over their heads. "Don't look up."

Summer laughed as a soft rain of salty water streamed over their bodies, rinsing away the last of the sand and leaving their skins smelling like the sea.

"That was an elegant solution," she said, smiling.

After another warm-water rinse to remove the traces of salt Michael gathered the bowls of herbs and roots, but took them into the pool room.

"Pagan, can you warm the bath?"

Troy sent another surge of his power into the stone tub, which instantly melted the surface ice. Michael then emptied the bowls into the pool, and stepped down into it to stir the steaming water.

"That is brilliant," Summer said as she smiled and came to the edge. "How did you know to do it?"

"You said they use baths as medicine," the big man reminded her as he reached up to grip her waist. "Why scrub themselves with the dry herbs when they can soak in the hot water with them?"

Troy closed the door to the bath house before he came to join them. "I can smell the flowers and the ginger root, but what is that soft, deeper scent?"

"Sandalwood, maybe," Summer said. Slowly she stretched out to submerge her upper body, and braced her neck against a recess in the pool edge. "Oh, this is lovely. After all that scouring every inch of me feels squeaky clean." She breathed in and exhaled slowly. "We have another problem besides Meng. Elettra is falling in love with Cyrus."

"As he's already smitten with her," Troy said, "that's convenient." He took hold of Summer's foot and worked his thumbs against the arch. "And a disaster in the making."

"Shelton behaves like a prisoner, not a Templar," Michael said as he lifted Summer and slid behind her, shifting her onto his thighs.

41

"Have you noticed how he looks up at the sun as if it were something glorious and yet alien to him? Then he is always protective of Beauty and Elettra, when he should despise them. You saw how he was when the Fae fought with him."

"Bowers is the one he really hates," Troy said. He paused and looked up. "Do you think he was forced by the order to join the mission?"

"He is under some form of duress or control," Michael said. "If I can get him away from Bowers, perhaps he will confide in me." He smoothed back Summer's wet hair, and traced the curve of her bottom lip. "Until we know more, we should keep Elettra away from him."

Summer nipped his finger. "Killing a stone tiger might be easier." The foot massage Troy was giving her sent little jolts of sensation streaking up her legs. "What are you doing down there, you wicked man?"

"Guess," he said.

He bent his head and kissed each one of her toes before he took the smallest between his lips and sucked on it.

"Oh," Summer gasped. The sensations grew hard and hot, and made Summer grip Michael's forearms as she felt Troy's tongue tease a space between her toes. "I didn't know my feet were so, ah, Michael—"

"Every part of you belongs to us," the big man murmured to her. "Troy loves your feet, and your ear lobes, and that spot just above your navel. I have dreams about the bend of your knees, the curves of your palms, and the small of your back. I imagine kissing you there, and feeling you shake as I do." His voice went deeper. "And then we take you while you are soft and wet and needing us, like you are now."

Summer reached up to touch Michael's jaw, and felt him turn his face so that his mouth brushed over the soft pad of flesh just below her fingers. When his tongue swept across the center of her palm she felt a delicious ache pool between her thighs.

"Now would be terrific," she said, feeling her nipples puckering.

"So impatient," Troy said as he released her foot and caught the other between his hands. "Slow down. The night is ours."

The heat of the fragrant water and the lush caresses her lovers gave her combined to infuse Summer with a sudden, savage need.

"I can't," she said, her voice shaking, and felt a touch of fear. "Is it sex magic again?"

"No, love," Troy said as he stroked her calf.

"It's just us."

If her dark warlock didn't sense any enchantment, then Summer knew what she had to do. She pushed herself upright, centering herself over Michael's rigid erection so she could impale herself on him. Troy rose to his feet and gripped his shaft as he moved closer, cradling the back of her head as he guided her parted lips to his swollen cockhead.

"It's all right, love," Troy crooned softly as she engulfed him with her mouth. "Take what you need from us, yes, like that."

Beneath her Michael thrust, filling her tight, throbbing pussy with his full length.

"Fuck yourself on me while you suck him," he told her, his big hands covering her breasts and squeezing them in time with the rise and fall of her movements on him. "Pagan dreams of this, too—working himself between your soft lips while he feels my cock go deep. It makes him harder to know I am plowing your pussy."

The water in the pool sloshed as Michael lifted her and stood, supporting her torso with his arm as he plunged into her, pushing her mouth onto Troy with each hard stroke. The dark warlock wedged his hands under her as she sucked him, and shifted her back onto Michael. Back and forth she went until wild need blossomed as if to swallow her whole.

She could feel her breasts bouncing as she moved between them, and heard the slap of Michael's strong thighs against the back of hers. The herbs in the pool flooded her senses with some dark, carnal heat she'd never before felt. It stoked her pleasure, and she moaned around Troy's thick girth as the first burst of delight consumed her, and then another.

Troy's thighs went rigid, and he gripped her tightly as he shuddered and groaned. She swallowed each jet of his cream, relishing the taste and smell of his pleasure, releasing him with a wail.

"Beauty," Michael moaned and turned her while he remained planted deep in her clenching softness.

Troy held her from behind as the big man fucked her to another climax. The gripping spasms of her body wrenched a low rumble of relief from Michael as he jerked and flooded her with his silky come.

Somehow her mates lowered her together back into the water, where they held her as she shook and gasped through the violent aftershocks. Their mating had been so primitive Summer felt almost timid when she looked up into Michael's eyes.

"I'm sorry," she said, still panting as she pushed some damp strands of hair from her face. "I don't know what that was, but it kind of took charge."

"We have been abstaining a little too much, I think." He cradled her damp cheek and smiled with intense masculine satisfaction. "It was necessary. That is all that matters."

Troy kissed the top of her head. "And if you need it again, we're fine with it."

They soaked a little longer before drying off, dressing in the robes and returning to the main house. On the way to their rooms they passed Meng's servant, who bobbed as she bowed to them before hurrying away again.

"I think we scare her more than the stone tigers," Summer said as they went into their room. The prospect of cramming herself with her mates into the restricted space of the cabinet bed didn't appeal to her, so she reached to tug out the mattress. A small strip of red paper fluttered to the floor. She picked it up. "What do you think this is?"

Michael took it from her and examined the characters that had been inked on it. The paper suddenly dissolved into smoke.

"Something we were not meant to read, I

think."

"It was a talisman," a female voice said. "Protection, for your lady wife."

Summer turned to see the servant standing in the doorway.

"You put it here?"

The servant nodded and glanced over her shoulder.

"If you tell the master," she said quickly, "he will be angry." She tugged at a broken half of a coin she wore on a thong around her neck. "He does not believe in the old ways."

"But you do," Summer said and carefully approached her. She held out her hands. "Thank you."

The servant gripped her wrists. "Never be alone here, my lady. Never where your men cannot see you. Xishan will have you taken and put in his pleasure room. There you will be made to serve him, and he will pester you until you are broken or he finds another. The watchmen will take you in a sack and drown you in the river."

"How do you know all that?" Troy asked her.

The woman's eyes glittered with tears. "It is what he did to my daughter, Luli. It is what he does with all the beauties that capture his eye. Xishan is not a man. He is a demon."

47

CHAPTER FOUR

"ATWATER, WAKE UP."

Troy opened his eyes to see Elettra standing over him in her Fae form, her long golden hair spilling over her flawless shoulders. Behind her Shelton stood looking furious. Before he could speak she shook her head, and bent lower.

"Bowers is gone, and so are Meng and his serving wench," Elettra murmured, placing a pile of clothes on the bed. "Guards are searching the house." Her goddess-like beauty vanished under a cascade of tiny stars as she resumed her mortal guise. "We will keep watch in the hall while you dress."

By then Summer and Michael were awake, and quickly put on the garments the Fae woman had brought. The dark, wide-sleeved silk robes and trousers fit Troy and his sentinel brother perfectly, as did the embroidered pink and red skirt, blouse and jacket meant for Summer.

"Here is some overnight magic," Michael said as he tied the ornate belt of his robe. "These were made for us."

"Do you think Meng reported us to the governor?" Summer asked.

"Either he or Bowers did," Troy said and felt the frustration of not knowing burn in his gut. "I imagine we'll find out soon enough."

Once they joined Elettra and Shelton in the hall Troy looked down from the landing to see a stern-faced man dressed in red and black climbing the stairs. A dozen watchmen with their swords drawn followed him.

"Did you see Bowers leave with Meng?" Troy asked the Templar.

Shelton shook his head. "They were gone when Elettra woke me. Are we to fight?"

"Not if we are to maintain our ruse of being the emperor's emissaries," Troy said. He glanced at the women. "But if it comes to that, stay out of our way."

Shelton moved to join Michael, whose serene expression indicated he was ready for battle. Troy made a gesture for everyone to be still as the stern-faced man approached them. He stopped a few feet away.

"What is the meaning of this?" Troy demanded.

"I am Guozhi, commander of the quarter watch," the man said flatly as he took a short scroll from his sleeve and unrolled it. "By order of the mighty Xishan, governor of Huaxian and the kingdom of earth, the emissaries from Peking are charged with trespass." He rolled up the scroll and replaced it before he regarded Troy. "We have been ordered to take you in our custody and escort you to the palace."

"These charges are false," Troy countered. "We were invited to stay here last night by Master Meng. We are guests of this house."

"Your trespass is not against the jeweler. It is posted at the gates that those who reside beyond the city are not permitted to remain within the walls after sunset. We are to take you to the palace, willing or not, so that the great Xishan may decide your fate." Guozhi tucked his hands into his sleeves. "You may go with us in peace, or in pain, but deliver you to the governor we will."

Troy saw the determination in the man's dark eyes, and nodded. "We will not resist."

From Meng's house the watchmen marched them through the city's streets, where every citizen who saw them quickly and deliberately looked away. Troy guessed it was not from disgust but terror, as if staring would result in them being arrested as well.

Summer moved between him and Michael and took their hands in hers.

Bowers may have followed Meng to the palace, and gotten himself arrested there, she thought through their telepathic link.

Or he escaped when he saw the guards coming into the house, Troy thought back, and felt a surge of disgust from Michael. *If he did, don't judge him too harshly, Paladin. You might have done the same when you were a Templar.*

Without warning he abandoned us and his brother in arms. Michael's jaw tightened. *Templar or not, I would never sacrifice another to save my own hide.*

Whether Bowers is inside or not, Troy thought, *we'll at least have a chance to search the palace.*

Guozhi led the procession to a wide canal, over which a curving stone bridge ran. On the other side was a towering, three-arched bronze gate in an even higher blue-brick wall. Troy noted the palace guards posted at both ends of the bridge as well as flanking the gate. Every man wore a hide mask painted to resemble a snarling reptile, and held two swords crossed over their chest armor.

"The magnificent Xishan is guarded by a thousand dragon warriors," Guozhi said as he bowed to the guards before starting across the bridge. "Should you attempt to escape, they will take your heads."

He means that, Summer thought, her emotions dark with fear and revulsion.

When Troy followed the direction of her gaze he saw the bundles of rotting, decapitated heads that had been hung by their long hair over the palace moat. Like ghastly ornaments, they dangled from the tree limbs by the hundreds.

"May we speak to the governor?" he asked the commander.

Guozhi scowled. "The resplendent Xishan allows no one in his presence but those beloved to him: his wife, his concubines, and his most trusted advisor."

Once they had crossed the bridge the watchmen abruptly stopped, parting on either side to turn and file back over the bridge. Palace guards took their place, surrounding Troy and the others in a precise square of eight with a ninth walking ahead through the left arch. Inside the gate a group of older women with pale faces stood waiting, and fell into step behind the two guards at the rear.

Despite the circumstances Troy felt a reluctant admiration for the palace's sumptuous interior. The governor had commissioned stunning artworks and adornments to cover literally every inch of the colorful rooms. Even the floors had been beautifully tiled to resemble water, grass, and even meadows of wildflowers. Small braziers smoldered, adding musky notes of incense and herbs to the soft air. In the sky well rooms, stone benches offered resting spots by ornate fountains and recessed bronze columns from which ferns and ivy spilled like green lace.

Guozhi came to a halt, turned right and entered a wide courtyard filled with pottery statues of richly-dressed women with impassive expressions and comically small features. Each statue had been made differently to appear as individuals, and the pottery had been painted to make the skin, hair and garments appear more life-like. In the center of the terra cotta court stood a small, airy throne. Its back panel of silk was framed with gold and edged with wood and jewels polished to a glassy finish.

A woman sat primly on the throne working languidly at a small, stretched panel of embroidery. She wore a gown so heavily encrusted with jewels that her entire body shimmered each time she took a breath. Her long hair had been drawn up to curve in a soft black wave around her white face. More jewels sparkled from the combs and sticks holding the intricately woven bun at her crown, and tiny golden chains looped along the edges of her delicate ears. Her mouth had been painted with vermillion, but only in the center, giving the effect of a crimped, bee-sting pout.

Although the lady sat up a little straighter, she did not look at Guozhi as he approached and prostrated himself in front of her.

"Lady Wu," he said, his voice muffled by the courtyard tiles, "forgive our intrusion on your peace, but we have brought the emissaries as the glorious Xishan, your husband, commanded."

The governor's wife continued stitching for a long moment before she set aside her needlework and stretched out her thin hands. Two serving women rushed to either side of the throne and bowed before her. They quickly locked their arms together and lowered themselves to the base of the throne. Lady Wu gracefully shifted from her seat onto the women's arms, and they carried her forward, lifting her over Guozhi and halting when they came to the guards in front of Troy.

Bright black eyes surveyed the dark warlock

with a sweeping look.

"Greetings, Emissary," Lady Wu intoned. "Our esteemed Xishan has put you in my charge while you stay with us." She nodded at Summer. "We are told that this female is wife, and yet she serves as concubine to you and another. What is she?"

Troy decided to tell her the truth. "My friend Michael and I are Lady Summer's lovers and protectors. Among our people we are the same as husbands and wife."

Wu's mouth pursed, emphasizing the circle of her lip paint.

"Men may have many wives and concubines here, but for a woman to be permitted two husbands… I have never heard of that."

"I apologize if our ways offend you," Troy said and wrapped his hand around Summer's. "But our lady is very dear to us, and we don't wish to be parted from her."

When Michael took Summer's other hand, the governor's wife shifted her gaze to his face.

"You are both of you very possessive with your shared wife. How is it that you feel no jealousy toward your friend when you are intimate? Or is there some other pillow arrangement?"

The big man smiled a little. "Troy and I care for each other as brothers, not lovers."

"That is very interesting to me. My parrot proved quite confused by your arrangement." Lady Wu wrapped her fan against one of her bracelets, and the servant from Meng's house trotted into the courtyard. "I see now your muddle, Parrot. I will not have you whipped for stupidity after all."

The woman bobbed up and down in mute gratitude, but when she caught Troy's stare she shook her head slightly.

The governor's wife inspected Shelton, who stood close behind Elettra.

"You are too large and strong to be pleased by such a small, dull female. Why do you not share the jewel-eyed one as well?"

"He is celibate," Elettra said before he could reply. "And I am not dull."

Lady Wu's lips curved. "As I see."

"Lady Wu," Summer said, "we are grateful for your kindness, but may we be permitted to return to Meng's house? We would not wish to impose on the governor's hospitality."

"You did that when you came into the city," Wu told her.

"Then may we speak to the governor?" Troy asked. "We would appreciate a chance to explain our mission to him."

"No," she said flatly. "My husband left public life to find serenity some five years past, and now does not wish his tranquility disturbed." She sighed as she reached down and rubbed the side of her tiny foot. "The incomparable Xishan has not yet made clear his intentions toward you. Until he illuminates us with his wisdom, you may not leave the palace."

"I see," Summer said and glanced down to where Lady Wu was massaging her foot. "Forgive me, but are you injured, my lady?"

"I am made beautiful," the governor's wife said and removed her delicate slipper. Tightly-knotted silk bandages encased a tiny, pointed foot only a few inches long. "You do not follow the path of the lotus?" she asked. When Summer shook her head Wu lifted a perfect brow. "Among our people women of rare beauty must have small feet."

"Even if they are in terrible pain?" Summer asked.

"We endure what we must," Lady Wu said, looking thoughtful. "I was one of the fortunate ones. My mother began wrapping my feet when I was an infant, and my bones were soft. By the time I married I attained perfection. My lord husband was most gratified."

Troy suddenly understood why the serving women carried her from her throne.

"You can't walk," he said, "can you?"

"A little, if I wish, but there are always servants to attend me." She gazed at every part of Summer's face, lingering on her eyes. "Parrot was correct in her description of you. The eyes of an empress." Then she glanced down. "But the feet of a peasant. Put me back now."

The serving women carried Lady Wu back to the throne, and gently placed her on the seat.

"Forgive my intrusion, my lady," Meng said as he appeared beside her. He leaned down to murmur something. She in turn spread a fan and held it up to cover their faces.

"Master Meng," Shelton said and took a step forward. He halted when Lady Wu made a stopping gesture at him. "We have been separated from Brother Bowers. Have you seen him, Master Meng?"

The jeweler ignored him as he said something in a sharper tone to the governor's wife, who closed her fan and swatted him with it. Indignation flickered across Meng's features before he turned and stalked out.

"Those who serve should do well to remember their place," Lady Wu said, her eyes bright with anger as she stared after him. She glanced at the guards. "Escort the emissaries to the Hall of Serene Dawn."

• • • • •

Once they were shown to their rooms in the very back of the palace's inner court, Summer and her mates were separated from Elettra and Shelton, who were taken to the end of the corridor. She and Elettra exchanged a look before the guards ushered them into their respective chambers.

"You need not worry," Michael told her, as the guards closed and bolted the door. "Shelton will die before he allows anyone to harm her."

She had to smile a little. "I know," she said quietly.

As she surveyed their quarters, she wrapped her arms around her waist and tried to find something about the room to like.

All the bright, violent colors used for the décor represented every hot shade of the spectrum, and blazed around her like silent fires. Boldly painted scenes of battles and conquests covered the walls, and sculptures and statues of menacing, snarling dragons occupied nearly every flat surface. Even the furnishings, rich and ornate as they were, sported carvings and paintings of predatory animals baring their teeth and claws.

"What do they call this style? Early Chinese Violence?" she said, and caught Troy watching her. "Sorry. This isn't exactly a restful place, is it?"

"No, but if we try to leave, the dragon men will lop off our heads, or the stone tiger patrol will eat us in the streets." He looked up at the writhing snakes that had been painted on the ceiling. "Maybe it's a sensory torture chamber."

"Good, then it's not just me," Summer said and perched on a padded bench. "I wonder if Meng knows he has a spy in his house."

"I don't think Parrot is a spy, exactly," Troy said and sat down beside her. He told her how the servant had looked at him while bowing to Lady Wu. "Maybe I'm reading into it, but it felt like a warning to me. I also think the story about her daughter was true."

Michael tried the door, which was locked from the outside, and then knelt down and looked through the gap at the bottom.

"Two guards in the hall," he said as he crossed the room and looked out through the thick wooden slats covering the window opening. "Ten in the courtyard outside." He glanced at Troy. "That woman knew too much about us. Bowers must have betrayed us to Xishan."

"I'm not so sure about that," Troy told him. "He might have seen the watchmen coming, and simply slipped out before they arrived. He does seem to know a great deal about Chinese history and culture, so maybe he knew where to hide."

Michael uttered a sour sound. "Or he betrayed us and is dining with Xishan now."

Summer felt the bright brush of Elettra's thoughts.

"Quiet, please," she murmured.

She focused on the mind link they shared.

Are you and Shelton safe?

For now, yes. Summer, the Fae woman thought to her. *I could not tell you in front of that crippled woman, but TerraCairn is here inside the palace. As soon as they brought us inside it called to me directly.*

Summer felt a cautious surge of relief. *So Wickerman hasn't gotten to it yet. Can you track it now?*

As soon as we are free to move about, yes. I will speak to you later.

Elettra ended the link so abruptly that Summer blinked. She passed the thoughts along to her mates, touching a finger to her lips as she did so. If the governor had used a servant to spy on Meng, there was no telling who was listening in on them inside the palace.

"Why don't we take a nap?" she said. "I'm tired."

The palace's cabinet-bed was much larger and grander than Meng's, and once they climbed inside it her mates stretched out on either side of her. The feather-stuffed mattress sank under their weight, and smelled faintly of a strange, smoky herb, but its softness was cloud-like and warm. Summer had intended to go on discussing their situation with her mates through their link, but to her surprise she grew genuinely drowsy.

"Do you think Lady Wu spiked our bed with sleeping herbs?" she asked.

"I think you're just worn out," her dark warlock said and pressed his mouth to her brow. "Close your eyes. We'll wake you in a few hours."

Troy and Michael snuggled closer and folded their arms over her. In moments Summer drifted off into the warmth and safety of their embrace. For a time she dozed, and then fell into a deeper sleep, only to awake in Lady Wu's courtyard of terra cotta ladies. This time the elegant throne held a small white lamb cuddled on a pile of dark green silk. The little animal raised its head and regarded her with bright emerald eyes.

Summer knew that the Emerald Tablet enjoyed manifesting itself in her dreams as animals, but it always had a purpose. Troy and Michael appeared and came to stand beside her.

"Why have you summoned us?" Summer asked the lamb. "We know we're in danger."

You are blind to the scope of it, the Emerald Tablet said, and rose on its thin legs to leap down from the throne. *You think only of your dreams, and not those of others.*

Summer felt exasperated. "How can I know what others dream?"

Accept nothing you see. Look instead for what is hidden all around you. The lamb butted its head against one of the terra cotta figures. The pottery cracked and fell away from a large hole in the skirt. Inside the dried clay a discolored leg bone gleamed. *This is what is done to those who displease the mistress of this place. You must not anger her.*

Summer went to the broken figure, and peered into the hole.

"There's an entire skeleton in here," she said and quickly straightened. "Why would she kill her own servants?"

"I don't think they were serving her," Troy said. He went over to one statue that wore a broken half-coin around her neck. "Maybe Luli never actually made it to the river."

The dream of the courtyard spun away, and

Summer turned to find herself standing in the
meadow outside Troy's house in the White
Mountains of New Hampshire. Her mates lay
sleeping in the wildflowers, and when she moved
to join them the white lamb hopped in front of
her.

This time is ours alone, Daughter.

Summer crouched down beside the lamb, which
butted her chest with its blunt little head.

"You can't crack me open, I'm afraid."

I do not wish to break you. The voice inside her
mind chilled. *The crystal of earth does.*

The air turned dark and murky as a streak of
pale gold light blasted up through the clouds from
the west. The solid column of power streaked
higher and higher, disappearing into the upper
stratosphere like a rocket. Summer thought it
would fade, but suddenly a violent burst of light
made her shield her eyes with her hand.

High above the planet, the moon erupted with
a powerful blast, splitting it into four pieces as the
power engulfed it.

Summer had seen the aftermath of the
destructive force in her first dream of the
Apocalypse. The destroyed moon had begun
raining down on the black ruin of the lifeless
planet. But somehow knowing that TerraCairn

was directly responsible terrified her even more.

"Is that why you are showing me this? To warn me of how powerful it is?"

No, Daughter. This vision is neither yours nor mine. The lamb looked up at the broken moon. *This is TerraCairn's dream.*

• • • • •

Elettra watched Shelton wrench down a silk tapestry to wrap it around his hips.

"You need not do that. The serving wench said she would bring back mended clothes for us."

As they'd entered their chamber, one of the guards had shoved her. Before she could stop Shelton, he'd had the man on the floor. But when all of the guards had drawn their blades at once, he'd had to relent.

"They didn't need to take our clothes," he said. He turned around, stared at her naked body for a moment, and then showed her his back again. "Take a sheet from the bed and cover yourself."

"If you had not been so surly," she said, "the guards would never have torn them as they did. It was meant to humiliate us."

Elettra sat down on the edge of the bed and picked up a small sculpture of gems from a nightstand. Without the inclusions and flaws the stones might have been uncut Fae crystal.

"You can look at me, you know," she said, putting the sculpture back. "Even when I am unclothed my mortal guise is like a garment."

"It is not proper," he said and went over to the window of their chamber.

Since he was ignoring her Elettra decided to inspect the room. She found several more objects of the odd crystal to keep her occupied, but her gaze kept straying back to the Templar. Shelton's largeness and muscular bulk pleased her, for he resembled the men of her race more than the others. He could never be called handsome, not with that bold nose and brooding brow, but she approved of his rugged features as well. The only thing she questioned was the metal thing around his thigh that dug into his flesh. But when she looked into his smoky dark eyes something always knotted in her belly—and not unpleasantly. Now that Elettra had seen his manhood the sensation returned, for Shelton proved to be as big there as the rest of him. She eyed the knot of gems in her hand and quickly placed it on the table.

"Have you ever mated with a woman?" she asked. His broad shoulders stiffened, but he remained silent. "I never did with a man," she said, wandering back to the bed. "No one in my birth clan wanted me because I was never angry, or vengeful, or even unhappy. Visitors to our stronghold were told I was simple, so they too avoided me. When I was imprisoned at the Fae King's court I feared that Devalan's sire might force himself on me, but he seemed content with daily beatings." She touched her face. "Most of the women of my clan were far prettier, so perhaps that is—"

Shelton strode over to her, hauled her to her feet, and shook her. "Stop it."

His flushed face and hard grip made Elettra drop her mortal guise so she could face him on eye level.

"Stop what?"

"Talking about yourself like that," he said. "Talking, looking at me, wondering, wanting." He cradled the back of her skull with his big hand as he looked all over her face. "You are driving me mad."

Elettra felt astonished by how suddenly he had gone from remote and bored to hot and angry. His large manhood pressed against her belly like a thick iron rod, and his fingers no longer dug into her flesh but caressed it. Her own body had grown heavy and tingled all over. The throbbing, wet emptiness between her legs would soon become unbearable. He wanted to mate with her, and apparently she wanted the same.

"I am confused," she admitted, her voice curiously thready. "You said you do not do this."

Shelton released her and started to turn away. When she made a soft sound of protest he swung back around and tackled her.

They fell onto the edge of the bed, where Shelton pinned her down with his heavy frame and began putting his mouth on her breasts. He pinned her wrists down as he kissed and licked and sucked at her, his mouth hungry and greedy and so, so good. She arched her back to press one puckered nipple against his lips, and he enveloped it, sucking and lashing it with his tongue until she thought she would scream.

Shelton lifted his head and stared into her eyes as he shifted, pressing the long ridge of his erect penis against the slick ache between her thighs.

"I want to do this," he growled. He stroked the bulge against her, and her wetness dampened the silk covering him. "I want to be inside you, and have you, and pump myself into you until I fill your lovely golden pussy with my seed."

What was he waiting for?

"Cyrus?"

"I dream of it," he muttered, pushing harder against her soft mound. "How it would feel, and the sounds you might make, and the pleasure we could share. I dream of it even when I am awake. I want to fuck you, Elettra GemSage, in every way I can, for as long as I can, until neither of us can move."

She nodded, eager to begin. "Now, please?"

He shuddered, burying his face in her hair for a moment before he pushed himself away from her and retreated. For a long time Elettra lay there staring at the inside of the cabinet bed and wondering if she might kill him for not mating with her. It would not be difficult. She was much stronger than he. One blow to the base of the skull ought to do the work. And why were there tears in her eyes now, brimming and threatening to spill down her face?

"It will not happen," Shelton said from where he stood at the window. "It cannot."

"If that is your wish," she said, her voice unsteady. Slowly Elettra sat up and gathered the sheet around her as she shifted back into her mortal guise. "Can you teach me what you do?"

He gave her a blank look. "Summer will not share her mates, and like these people Bowers is too small for me. So it seems that I must be celibate, too. Is it that thing around your leg that chafes your skin? Perhaps you could make one for me."

He looked as if he might lunge at her again, but she snatched up the sculptured gems and hurled them across the room. She watched them sail past his head and smash against the wall with a burst of light.

"The next one will not miss," she said.

CHAPTER FIVE

LADY WU'S SERVANTS woke Summer and her mates with a soft rap on the door. They silently brought in a morning meal for them, and set it out on a low table before bowing and retreating. After watching TerraCairn smash the moon to pieces at the end of her dream Summer didn't feel especially hungry, but sat with her men and nibbled on a small, fried rice ball as they ate.

Troy held a chunk of smoked fish out to her, and then frowned when she shook her head.

"You haven't eaten since last night, since Meng's house," he said. "You need something in your stomach before we face the dragon lady and her magnificent husband."

"Don't be disrespectful of our hosts," she said, nodding at the door where she was sure the guards were listening to every word they said.

I need to show you something.

Through their bond link Summer replayed the end of her dream. Sharing the Emerald Tablet's final revelation with Troy and Michael made her feel a little guilty. Her lovers had enough to worry about with the here and now. But it also helped to feel their love and strength once she had.

Knowing they were being a little too quiet, Summer said out loud, "I wonder if we'll dine with Lady Wu later. I don't think she means to keep us locked in here all day."

"We could tell her about the survey we are making of Shaanxi," Michael said. His gaze shifted over her shoulder. "Now, if you wish, my lady. Please, join us."

Summer's eyebrows arched as the governor's wife emerged from behind a carved wood and silk screen. Though it had appeared to serve as a decoration against the wall, it concealed the entrance from an adjoining room. She looked as smug as ever, her petite form this time nestled on the locked arms of two fat, nearly-naked men with oddly childish features.

"You have sharp eyes, Emissary," Lady Wu said.

Parrot carried a smaller version of her courtyard throne into the chamber, and placed it by the low table. Once the men placed her on the seat they stepped back, stopping only when their shoulders touched the wall.

"Do you not have eunuchs in your country, Emissary's Wife?" Lady Wu asked.

Summer cringed a little to be caught staring. "No, my lady. That is, I don't know about such practices."

"We cut and train young boys here so they might one day serve in noble households," Lady Wu said, sounding as if she were talking about trained animals. "No less than a dozen of our eunuchs have gone on to attend the imperial court. It is said the Jiajing prefers our stock above all others."

"Do their families place them in service?" Michael asked, sounding polite while curling his hands into bulging fists.

"The former governor purchased the boys from various villages, but my husband simply asks, and families bring their sons to us. Some beg that we show them our favor by castrating their dearest ones." Her bright eyes shifted to Summer's face as she motioned to the food. "Eat well, Emissary's Wife. Shortly you shall all enjoy a privilege granted to few."

Although she beamed at the three of them, the glitter of her dark eyes turned cold. A tiny shudder ran down Summer's spine.

"May we know of this privilege?" Troy finally asked.

Lady Wu favored him with a tiny nod. "You shall see the Hall of Military Eminence. My husband will pass sentence on you there."

• • • • •

As Troy marched next to Summer, Michael took up position on her other side. Behind them Elettra and Shelton followed close. The phalanx of guards that surrounded them was square, as before, but a few of them were a little smaller. Guozhi, commander of the quarter watch, led at the front.

We could take them, Troy thought to his sentinel brother.

Michael calmly glanced left and right. *Not without danger to Beauty.*

You can pull her away quickly enough, Troy thought, *I count three against nine.* He smirked. *It almost gives them a fighting chance.*

We're where we need to be, Summer broke in as they headed down the stairs. *The crystal is here somewhere.*

We're not going to find it if we're under house arrest, Troy countered. He glanced up at the sky as they entered the palace's deserted main compound. *Or if we're sentenced to death.*

"We are moving away from the crystal," Elettra said under her breath.

Troy gave her a brief nod. At least it was good to know it was still here. Wickerman and his cultists might not have had a head start, but Elettra had been completely sidelined—as had they all.

At the four corners of the enormous plaza stood the four black and red towers they'd seen from the plateau. They soared upward like sturdy sentinels, watching over everything for miles around. Only now did Troy realize that almost everything in the palace was that way.

Without warning the guard detail changed direction and headed toward an imposing building. Its light gold roof gleamed in the sun, sloping left and right over the massive structure, which was almost as wide as the entire wall behind it. Crimson columns the size of redwood trees supported the roof. An even wider set of stairs led up from the plaza to the base of the columns. The closer they got, the bigger the building seemed to get. By the time they reached the bottom step, they all had to crane their necks to look up.

At the top of the steps, gilded statues of seated lions were located every few yards. Some held a human victim in their mouth, while others rested a giant clawed paw on a prone body. From under the tiles of the roof, stone dragon snouts protruded. Cheek by jowl, they formed a continuous, snarling ledge that stretched from one end of the building to the other. As they passed under and entered the building proper, the floor became polished marble streaked with branching veins of gold. Their footsteps echoed off the immaculate surface as they entered the cavernous front room of the great hall.

"We need to find Meng," Shelton said, barely audible over the echoes of the boots of the guards. But when one of the guards turned his masked face toward the Templar, he quickly cleared his throat.

Troy considered the suggestion. It was true that Meng had seemed like an ally, only to pointedly ignore them in the presence of Lady Wu. But the machinations in the governor's palace were not something they would easily untangle.

If we find Meng, we might find Bowers, Michael thought.

If he's still alive, Troy thought back.

We can use all the help we can get, Summer put in. As they passed into a second room, they all instinctively gazed up. *Particularly now.*

The Hall of Military Eminence lived up to its name. It was three stories tall inside, with observation decks on every level. Torches blazed in hundreds of freestanding stanchions bordering the hall. But instead of massive columns ringing the enormous space, giant metal warriors stood at attention. As with the terra cotta versions they had already seen, each one of the dozens of stern soldiers was an individual. They stood with pikes, swords, bows, crossbows and axes. At their feet were bronze braziers carved like spiked mace heads. Long gray tendrils of incense smoke drifted upward, languidly playing across the soldier's rugged features. The movement almost made them seem alive.

But as with the plaza, Troy noticed that no one else was present—including on the ornate throne. Their footsteps quieted as they were marched onto a white carpet that swirled with curving green dragons who seemed to fly among stylized circles of clouds. Behind the red lacquered throne, a wide silk screen soared from floor to ceiling. Although the swirling dragon motif was repeated, it was done in silver threads on a white background, almost too faint to see.

Suddenly the phalanx stopped.

Summer looked around. "Where is the governor?"

Guozhi smartly executed an about face.

"We await the mighty Xishan," he barked.

In unison, his men spread their feet and planted their pikes in front of them. No one looked left or right. Nor did anyone say anything.

Troy shrugged. "Apparently we wait."

CHAPTER SIX

JADINE CUTTER DUCKED quickly into yet another storeroom. Since agreeing to lead the team back in time to retrieve the four treasures of the GemSage she had often felt she might fail the master. Wickerman had called her his greatest love, and his most lethal weapon, but she had never undertaken such a mission. At times she wished she had refused, but the moment she had looked into her lover's beautiful eyes she knew she would give her life to please him.

No other warlock had ever made her feel so cherished.

She smirked beneath her mask as she thought of her mother's grubby little country coven, and how they had always made her feel like a freak for her ability. Before she left for Pompeii, Wickerman had insisted she pay a visit to settle accounts with her former friends and family, telling her she would never know peace in her heart until she did.

"You are a marvelous woman, and the best fighter with a blade I have ever seen," the master had said as they lay naked and entwined in his bed. He had spent hours kissing every one of her scars. "That they forced you to become a rogue is the worst of injustices. Go and see to it that they can never harm you again, and then you can embark on this mission with a clear head and a healed heart."

Jadine had slipped into the coven house after everyone had gone to bed. It had taken her all night to dispatch her mother's circle, who had battered her with their abilities and then pleaded for their lives. One by one she'd killed them, thrusting her blades into each heart until only her mother was left.

"The Goddess forgive you," the old woman told her as she went down on her knees. "For I never will, Jadine. I should have ripped you from my womb before you could take your first breath."

"Being short-sighted does have its consequences."

Jadine had leaned down to kiss the top of her

head before she lopped it off with her sword.

Delivering her mother's head to Wickerman had made Jadine feel humble rather than proud. Without his love and understanding she would never have freed herself from her unhappy past.

Quickly, she rummaged through every shelf in the storeroom. If it took her a lifetime she'd find TerraCairn. No matter how many rooms, hellholes, or people she had to go through, she would find it. Then she would deliver it to Wickerman, just as she'd done with her mother's head.

• • • • •

If Summer had to stand a moment longer, she might fall. Though she had no idea how much time had passed, it felt like hours.

It has been hours, Michael thought to her. *You are meant to feel tired.*

Early on Michael had tried to support her, but Guozhi had forced them all to keep their distance and stand in order. Troy had explained why.

It's a standard softening technique, he'd thought to her. *They want to wear us down, and make us frightened.*

But if he's just going to sentence us to death, she'd thought back, *what does it matter?*

83

But now she could see why.

Above and all around them, the observation decks had started to fill. They appeared to be townspeople like the ones they'd encountered when they first reached Huaxian. Behind them Summer glimpsed guards who seemed to be herding them. Apparently the great Xishan wanted a great audience, and there was only one reason Summer could surmise: they were to be made an example.

"Guards!" Guozhi barked.

Summer started at the sudden sound, and put a hand to her chest when the soldiers all around them came to attention. The guards on the right made a quick right-face and marched off, while the guards on the left did the same, joined by Guozhi.

"At last," Elettra said, just behind her, "the wait is over. I have had enough waiting in my life."

Michael and Troy both put an arm around Summer's waist as she turned to the Fae woman. Shelton stood close to her as well. They looked as tired as she felt. It hadn't been just the standing and the silence. It was the not knowing.

A gong crashed from somewhere near the throne. Impossibly loud, it evoked a few cries of surprise from the galleries up above. Stunned faces turned toward the throne. But instead of seeing anyone approach the lavish high-backed bench, the floor-to-ceiling silk panel behind it illuminated. Apparently lit from behind, the white fabric stitched with swirling dragons eerily glowed. An awed gasp filled the hall.

"None may look upon my face!" a deep voice boomed.

The sound thundered all around them as Summer teetered on wobbly knees. Troy and Michael tightened their holds on her.

Suddenly a black shadow blossomed on the white silk screen behind the throne. A woman in the upper decks screamed as the gigantic figure of a man wearing some type of square hat loomed. It stretched upward until the shadow of his head hit the paneled ceiling and then crept along it.

"Some type of projection," Michael said.

Summer was about to agree until the eyes in the dark face on the ceiling flared white.

"Gods," she muttered.

More shrieks came from the gallery.

"Nice trick," Troy said.

"Why does the coward not show himself?" Elettra muttered.

"I wouldn't be too anxious for that," Shelton said.

"None is allowed to enter my city!" the voice proclaimed. Summer felt the deep booming bass in the souls of her feet and in the middle of her chest. It was an onslaught of sound. "The sentence for trespass is—"

"They are here by invitation!" a woman's voice yelled from somewhere behind them.

All heads turned and Summer knew her mouth must be hanging open. "Lady Wu?"

The same hushed name was on everyone's lips. The observers on the decks above rushed forward to the railing, pointing at her.

Riding on a black-lacquer palanquin that sparkled with mother-of-pearl inlay, Lady Wu moved forward carried by four large servants.

"Mighty Xishan," she called out. "Hear your humble servant!"

What is she doing? Summer thought to Troy and Michael.

Her bearers set down the litter, and the lady slowly stood. Her black silk gown was covered in so many pearls there was barely fabric showing. Each iridescent sphere seemed to reflect the flickering light of the myriad torches.

She is saving our lives, Michael thought.

But the question is why, Troy thought back.

"Your devoted wife," Lady Wu said, placing

both hands over her heart, "Lady of the Palace, and the Highest Consort begs Mighty Xishan's indulgence."

She performed a low and elegant bow.

All eyes returned to the looming giant and the bright eyes that stared from the ceiling. The quiet stretched on until someone in the gallery coughed.

"We grant it," the deep voice said, though the shadow never moved.

Although Summer couldn't be sure, its tone was a little less imperious.

Lady Wu straightened and gestured behind her without looking.

"These Imperial Emissaries and their wives were requested by your dutiful wife," she said. "They are to map the extent of your great kingdom. Let there be no doubt of its vast extent, both now and in future generations." She raised both hands to the throne. "To the mighty Xishan's glory!" Then she folded her arms across her chest. "This is your lady's gift to her majestic husband." She paused for a just a moment. "Should he permit it." She bowed again without rising.

The silence that followed was deep. As she, Troy, and Michael exchanged a look, she could hear Elettra and Shelton shift behind them. Even the fluttering of the torches around the room seemed loud.

"It is permitted," the bass finally rumbled.

Without knowing she'd held her breath, Summer let it go.

The glowing eyes on the ceiling winked out and the shadow immediately began to shrink. A furious buzzing of conversation filled the hall. As Lady Wu sat, she waved her hand at her servants then clapped her hands twice. Guozhi and his squad appeared from nowhere and surrounded them.

"So we are not dead," Elettra said, "but we are not free."

As Lady Wu's litter passed them, she caught Summer's eye. A satisfied smile crept across the woman's face.

"Why intervene on our behalf?" Shelton said as Guozhi took up position in front of the phalanx.

"I'm sure we'll find out," Summer said.

CHAPTER SEVEN

DESPITE THE DECOR, Summer found herself looking forward to returning to their room. Darkness had fallen, and with it a chill had returned. As expected, Elettra and Shelton were escorted back to their chamber. But when the guards opened the door to Summer, Troy, and Michael's room, a pleasant surprise waited. Gold trays with red lacquer bowls of food were everywhere. Before the door had even closed, Summer was sampling the most luscious slice of peach she had ever tasted, flavored with just a hint of ginger. The slices had been arranged like the petals of a flower, and at the center was some type of candied fruit. Summer quickly popped it in her mouth and sighed.

"Apricot," she murmured around the mouthful.

Michael was quickly devouring a joint of meat

that looked like fried chicken, while Troy was using his fingers to eat strips of beef half-covered with red paste. When Michael set down the bones, he poured three cups of tea and handed them out. They drank their cups in one long draught. Michael took them and poured again.

"Standing all day is thirsty work," Troy said with a grin, taking the refilled cup and quickly draining it again.

He picked up a pair of chopsticks and served thick brown noodles mixed with bok choy onto three plates. Michael added more chicken to his, while Summer put dried fish on her plate and Troys. They took their plates to the bed and sat on its edge.

"It is good to see you eat, Beauty," Michael said.

"It's funny how avoiding a death sentence improves the appetite," she said, before stuffing noodles in her mouth.

For several minutes they ate in silence and Summer felt a bit revived. Either it was the best tasting food she'd ever had, or she'd been starving.

Both, Troy thought to her, just as Michael thought the same thing.

Summer laughed a little and thought about a

second helping, but the door quietly opened.

Parrot led a group of servants bearing basins of steaming water, a stack of white cloths, and new garments.

"Lady Wu bids me to invite you to wash and change your clothes," she said, bowing and looking at the floor. She stood up and glanced over her shoulder at the guard who watched from the door. "When you are ready, you will be taken to the Room of Soft Sighs."

"We're perfectly comfortable here," Troy said.

But Parrot didn't reply. Instead she simply filed out with the rest of the servants, and the guard closed the door behind them.

"Honestly," Summer said, getting up and heading to the basins. "A wash sounds good right now."

Troy grinned at her. "I could help you with that."

"You finish eating," she said with a smile. "I think I can handle this."

She quickly stripped and dipped one of the soft cloths in the hot water. As she ran it over her skin, she marveled at how smooth it was—and soothing. But it was having the opposite effect on her mates, whose positively carnal thoughts came through loud and clear. She glanced at them sitting on the bed and both of them had stopped eating.

"I never tire of seeing you like this," Michael said.

"You may not have a choice," she replied, as she shook out one of the new garments.

Although the silk was incredibly soft when she put it on, it was sheer. She could easily see herself through it. Michael and Troy grinned at her.

"There are two more of these robes," she suggested, arching her eyebrows.

In no time, both her mates had stripped, washed, and donned their own see-through clothes. Summer took a moment to admire the hard, masculine lines of their bodies. Troy's form was chiseled, without an ounce of fat. While Michael's frame was huge and his muscles bulky.

Summer was musing on a few carnal thoughts of her own, when the door opened again.

"What timing," she said.

But when she realized that guards were filing into the room, she covered herself with her hands and retreated behind Michael and Troy. But none of the dragon men even glanced at her. Instead the one closest to the door motioned to it.

Though her cheeks were burning, Summer couldn't reach their other clothes. The guard motioned again. Although she grimaced, she reluctantly fell into line. With Michael in front of her and Troy behind, they made their way into the empty hall, passing the chamber where Elettra and Shelton were being kept.

Summer considered contacting her through their mind link, but what would she say? That they were passing by outside wearing almost nothing. Just a couple rooms down the guards came to a stop. The door in front of them was painted like the night sky. The dragon guard at the head opened it and stood aside.

The Room of Soft Sighs appeared to be an elaborate bed chamber, but thankfully didn't resemble their former quarters at all. Once they entered, the door closed behind them.

Thin white silk draped and covered the massive bed in the center of the floor, but it had been fashioned from a raised platform instead of the usual enclosing cabinet. One wall beyond it was mirrored with long, wide panels of brightly polished silver, and the opposite had been fashioned of jade carved with such detail it resembled a curtain of soft green lace. Small stone pedestals encircled the bed, and atop each one were objects fashioned from polished jewels that had been fused together.

"These are definitely worth sighing over," Summer said as she admired two interlocking circles made of bright green stones. When she touched the glittering facets they felt warm, startling her. "Michael?"

"They are not jewels," he murmured as he guided her hand away. "I can feel them. They are...very special crystals."

"They are pretty, but I don't sense any magic in them," Troy added in a low voice. "I think these may be the kind of sculptures Elettra has mentioned."

Since the Fae woman sculpted crystal into art forms, Summer felt a little reassured. Kember had come to Huaxian on the pretense of trading jewels.

"Perhaps one of her people brought them as tributes for the governor," she said.

"This reminds me of your eyes," Michael said as he picked up two pyramids of opal-colored crystal linked by a delicate clasp. He held it up beside Summer's face. "No, yours are more blue and brilliant, Beauty."

"You always make me feel so lovely," she said, feeling quite pleased. She took the opal sculpture and set it back on the pedestal before taking his hands and drawing him toward the bed. "Come here and admire more of me."

"Is that an open invitation?" Troy asked.

"You stay there," Summer said as she opened her robe. She allowed the edges to frame the inner curves of her breasts, while giving a glimpse of the silky, golden brown curls covering her sex. "I want you to admire us both," she said, surprising herself.

When she pushed the thin robe away from Michael's broad shoulders, he turned his head to kiss the back of her hand.

"Touch me," he said. "I need to feel your fingers on my skin."

"Just my fingers?" she teased as she moved closer, and let the pebbly beads of her nipples caress the hard muscles of his abdomen.

Troy groaned and rubbed his hand over his own belly. "He likes that very much."

Feeling almost giddy with love and desire, Summer moved around Michael, and then went to Troy, glancing back over her shoulder at her golden lover while she pushed her hands inside her dark warlock's robe.

"Close your eyes, Paladin," she ordered.

When she let her hand drift down and curl around Troy's painfully erect shaft, Michael gasped and shuddered, his big hand pressing against the bulge in his robe.

"Feel me touch him," Summer whispered, caressing the thick heat of Troy's cock, and knowing that Michael enjoyed every stroke as well through their link. When Troy tried to embrace her, she glided out of his reach, moving behind him while she kept him firmly in her grasp. "What do you want from me now, Pagan?"

"Everything you want to give me, love." His voice sounded almost slurred now. "No, wait. Paladin?"

Michael rubbed his hands over his face. "Something in here. An enchantment, perhaps. Pagan feels it through me." He dragged in a deep breath and shook his head. "Beauty, it is everywhere."

Through the mists of longing filling her senses Summer understood, but when she scanned the room she found no spells or enchantments. Only their physical need seemed to scent the air with arousal, and the aching throb of their deepest wanting was all that danced over her skin.

"We are the magic in here," she whispered to Troy, unable to stop her hands from moving over the smooth, taut muscles of his thighs. "It's coming from us."

He turned and scooped Summer off her feet,

carrying her to Michael, who helped him slip off her robe and place her naked on the bed. They moved to either side, their silk robes fluttering to the floor as they lay beside her, their bodies hard and hot and ready for her.

Summer's heightened senses became flooded with the scent of their bodies, the feel of their flesh, and the sound of their pounding hearts. She released a slow breath, and heard it echo in a sigh from the jade wall. She looked at the beautiful carvings just as a lamp briefly flared, and saw the glitter of Lady Wu's black eyes peering through the two narrow swirls.

Someone is watching us, Troy thought as he touched her lips with his. *Lady Wu?*

Through the jade, Summer thought as she kissed him. *We have to stop. I'm not going to— Oh, Troy, I hate that she's watching, but I want you and Michael so much.*

It's the same for us, love, her dark warlock thought. He dragged in a breath and shook his head as if to clear it. *Paladin, can you get off the bed?*

Michael started to edge away, only to groan as Summer reached out to grab him.

Not if Beauty keeps touching me.

I don't care, Summer thought as her self-control crumbled. She guided Troy's hand between her thighs. *She wants to see how we make love? Fine.* As he parted her folds and tenderly stroked her clit she arched her hips. *Penetrate me. I'm so empty inside.*

We should do outlandish things, and shock her, Michael thought to them. *Only all I can think is how much Pagan and I want to be inside you.*

Shame swamped Summer, compounded by their intense dislike of Lady Wu. Sex was only one component of their bond, but it was a powerful and passionate one—something they had always considered very private. She hated that the governor's wife considered their love-making some form of entertainment.

Don't think about her, Troy thought. *Think about us.* The dark warlock pushed two fingers deep into her softness, curling them as he rubbed her delicate inner sheath. *I can't stop myself from loving you, and neither can Paladin.*

Then don't, Summer thought and smiled up at him and Michael. *I'm yours here and now, as I always have been. I will be yours forever. Troy is right. Forget Lady Wu. Love me.*

• • • • •

Michael took no pleasure from being watched by Lady Wu, but as soon as Summer asked them to make love to her something ignited in his blood.

It felt almost like anger, and for a moment he feared it was, until it shifted and gathered in his groin, stiffening his cock to such rigid hardness he thought it had been encased in iron.

Troy and Summer felt his sensations, or suffered their own, because their hands reached for him, and the three of them embraced. Summer parted her lips for Troy's hungry kiss, and drew Michael's head down to her breasts.

"This is what I felt in the bath house," Summer told them, moaning as Michael lashed her throbbing nipples, and gasping as Troy pressed his fingers deeper into her pussy. "Now you feel it, too. Why is this happening?"

"We can stop it now," Michael said but knew he was lying. The desire hammering inside him felt as maddening and consuming as wildfire. "Troy and I will move away from you. We will find cold water and douse ourselves. We will...not. Beauty, I cannot bear it any more than you could in the pool."

Without hesitation Summer climbed up over Troy, presenting her bottom to Michael.

"Help him," she said to the dark warlock. Troy gripped Michael's shaft and guided him into the hot, slick tightness of her pussy. "Come into me, Paladin. Let me make you wet."

Michael's first thrust went so deep the three of them cried out together, and then he forced himself to stroke slowly in and out, covering every inch of his shaft with her soft, sweet essence. It took all his strength to withdraw from her, but then he took hold of Troy's swollen erection, and fitted his smooth cockhead to Summer's pussy.

"Go into her, Pagan."

Troy drove just as deeply, but once he had plunged into her to his root he held himself inside, pressing her writhing body against him before he reached for the tight curves of her buttocks. He tugged them enough to open her, presenting the rosy pucker of her bottom for Michael.

"She needs you, Brother," he said to Michael. "She burns for you."

As Michael pressed his own heavy cockhead to her clenching rosebud Troy released her and fisted Michael's shaft, helping him to work his way into the narrow channel. After several deep grunts and gentle pumps, Michael took possession of her sweet ass, and felt the press of Troy's cock against the delicate flesh that separated them. He looked down at his brother, who gave him a slow grin, and brought his big hands to grip her trembling bottom.

"She is all that we ever dreamed of," Michael said. "And ours to love and kiss and fuck every night, every day, forever."

Troy nodded. "Our lovely, sexy wife."

The wrenching relief of plowing into their woman together sent shockwaves through Michael, who felt the echoing sensations pouring into him from Troy. Nothing he had ever known as a Templar, when he had tried to slake his needs by furtively paying mortal females to take him to bed, could compare. He knew his brother felt the same aching joy, for none of Troy's Wiccan lovers had ever satisfied his dark desires until Summer had come to him. Now that they had finally made sense of the puzzle that they were, the final fit was this, this joining, this having.

He loved every part of his lady, but when he buried his heavy cock in her tight bottom he felt how much she loved him. The clamping she gave his full length, the whimper of delight that escaped her lips, and the voluptuous bounce of her curves against his lower belly betrayed her secret lust for him there. She loved it when he skewered her so completely that it squeezed them all, and that joy flooded him like a raging river.

"You will come on me," he groaned, as he

pounded into her, driving his cock in and out with deep, hard thrusts. "Come on us both. Show them, Beauty, show them your love for your husbands. Show them how we make you feel."

His Beauty let out a wail, and shook as her fevered climax exploded. Michael kept fucking her as deeply and surely as Troy, knowing she needed every hard inch to heighten the billowing, bursting sweetness. Her bliss had barely abated when she came again, this time twisting between them as if frantic, and that sent him over the edge.

Nothing felt as good as those last, heavy thrusts, or the shaking delight of pumping that first jet of cream into her tight bottom, all the while feeling Troy's cock jerking and spurting deep inside her gripping pussy. That they came together sparked one last surge of hot ecstasy for Summer, who shuddered helplessly against them, before they collapsed in a tangle of limp limbs and heaving chests.

"More of that might kill me," the dark warlock said, sighing the words. "But now I understand the name of the room."

"I just wish I knew where that came from," Summer said, sounding breathless and happily exhausted all at once. "Do you think we can move there and buy a house?"

"There is no place on earth or in heaven like this," Michael murmured, smoothing his hand over Summer's tousled hair. "It is as you said. We are what makes this magic."

A muffled sound made Michael lift his head, and when he saw movement behind the jade wall he forced himself from the bed. He walked over to peer through the openings in the carvings.

"Troy, someone is in there, but I don't think it is Lady Wu."

The dark warlock came to join him, and together they searched the jade wall until Troy found a latch. When he pressed it, the carving swung out, revealing Elettra and Shelton. They had been gagged and tied together.

Summer dragged a sheet around her, while Troy untied Elettra, and Michael dealt with Shelton's bonds. They helped them to their feet.

"What happened?" Summer asked.

"Lady Wu likes to play games," Shelton said. "She sat in there with us while you were in bed, and then her servants carried her out through a passage in the back."

"She said if we did not watch you that she would cut off our eyelids," Elettra said. "I like mine, so I watched. You and Troy and Michael are most impressive lovers." The Fae woman walked over to sit on the bed beside Summer.

The sculptures blocked our link, or I might have told you about the effect of the crystals.

Michael blinked at hearing Elettra's voice in his head. But before he could say anything, Lady Wu and her eunuchs came through the door, followed by the nine guards.

"You three do nothing special when you are intimate. My husband has more imagination, and he was a dog who chased every pretty bitch in the province." She touched a small distended vein in her temple. "Of course that was before he attained his serenity. Now he is the most excellent of husbands. As for you three, I am quite disappointed."

Summer rose to her feet, her eyes blazing with anger. "I'm sorry that we let you down, my lady."

Lady Wu tisked and waved her hand at Elettra and Shelton. "From the way they behave with each other I thought they might be virgins, in need of enlightenment." She made a dismissive sound and waved at the guards. "Escort them back to the guest rooms."

As they walked back from the Room of Soft Sighs, Elettra managed to move between Michael and Summer.

*I did not sense these crystals because they are tuned to
those who are not Fae, and only work if there are two or
more near them.*

So they weren't art sculptures? Summer thought
back to her. *We couldn't feel any magic coming from
them.*

*They are enchanted, but the spell transfers to anyone
who comes near them, so you would not sense it. They were
made to unveil and feed your desires from within you. That
is where their magic goes—into your body, where you
cannot detect it. They also blocked the link we share.*

Why would Kember leave behind something like that?
Michael thought to her through Summer's link.

Elettra and Summer stared at him in shock.

Perhaps the crystals did more than stoke our desires,
Michael thought and tapped the side of his head.
I can hear you both talking in my mind now.

So can I, Troy's wry voice said through the four-
way link.

I think I know why, Elettra thought and showed
Summer and her mates images of the crystal
sculptures. *Do you see the flaws in the stones? They are
proof that Kember did not bring them here. No Fae would
ever use or carry damaged crystal. It is unstable.* She saw
Summer's face. *Like Vesuvius.* She made an
explosive sound, and flung up her hands.

105

CHAPTER EIGHT

AFTER A BLISSFULLY dreamless sleep, Summer, Troy, and Michael had awoken with first light. They dressed silently, more aware than ever that they were likely being watched. As if to confirm it, Guozhi entered on cue.

"You are summoned to attend Lady Wu in her tea chamber," he said. Troy and Michael both scowled when the guards blocked their exit. "Only the Emissary's Wife," Guozhi ordered.

"I am honored by Lady Wu's kindness," Summer said out loud.

I'll be all right, she thought to them. *For some reason we're valuable to her, if only so she can watch us.*

I don't like you being alone with her, but all right, Troy thought and came to kiss her. *Keep the link open so we know what's happening.*

Michael did the same. *If you have to escape, hide*

and we will come for you.

The nine guards marched Summer to the center hall of the inner court, which proved to be a gallery of drawings and paintings of the same man. Assuming the subject was Xishan, Summer studied the governor's face. Each artist had depicted him in heroic fashion, either dueling or leading his dragon men into battle. But there was something odd about his eyes. Just as she reached her destination Summer realized what it was.

In every portrait Xishan's eyes had been painted a bright, unrealistic yellow, with the slit pupils of a feline.

Lady Wu's tea chamber turned out to be yet another grand ceremonial room. Every surface had been covered in blue and green silk embroidered with pearls of every shade imaginable, set in lines to resemble a rain shower. On the low black table, which had been inlaid with gold and jewels, a porcelain tea service had been placed to one side. A small mountain of fruit on a tray had been arranged to resemble the loess plateau, complete with a miniature of the doomed village.

Summer sat down on the pillow the lead guard indicated, and watched as Lady Wu was carried to hers from the opposite hall by two dragon men.

"Good morning, my lady."

"I am pleased to see you, Emissary's Wife," Lady Wu said as she arranged her pale orange robes.

Summer smiled at the servant who came to pour her tea before she nodded at the fruit sculpture.

"This is lovely," she said.

"Leave us," Lady Wu ordered. Once the guards and servants withdrew the governor's wife regarded her with a knowing smile. "Your two husbands are much besotted with you. While your love-making disappointed me, I felt quite envious of the declarations they made. Such devotion makes the burdens of marriage feel lighter in one's heart."

Summer wondered if she was envious. "You seem very fond of your husband."

"The great Xishan may call me wife, but his devotion belongs to our court magician." Lady Wu selected a persimmon slice from the tray and dropped it into a bowl of honey. "That I might better serve my lord husband I placed Parrot in the magician's household."

"Meng is the court magician?" Summer asked, her heart clenching, as she felt the twin echoes of dread through her link with Michael and Troy.

"Oh, yes," Lady Wu said. "He has served the wondrous Xishan for many years now." She flicked her hand back at the hall. "My husband was so enamored of Meng's creations that he ordered every single one kept in the palace treasure room."

Summer shook her head, took a sip of her bitter brew, and cleared her tight throat.

"I am honored in your trust, my lady, but I admit I am confused as to why you confide in me."

The governor's wife plucked her persimmon slice from the honey, and held it out as she might a treat for a well-behaved pet.

"Try this. It is a special delight of mine." Summer leaned forward and took it from her, then took a bite. Lady Wu smiled. "I know you possess great power, Emissary's Wife. Meng foretold your coming, you see. I have had you watched since you dropped from the sky."

Summer quickly chewed and swallowed. "Then why have you pretended otherwise?"

"It does no good to reveal myself to Meng. He simpers at me, but I know he has been looking for an excuse to kill me since he helped my husband find his tranquility." The governor's wife watched her face. "Even now I suspect he is convincing Xishan that you are demons sent to destroy our city, and that you must be executed. My powers have been limited by Meng's influence over my husband. If I am to help you avoid a very unpleasant death, you must do something for me."

Here it is, Summer thought to her mates. *This is the reason she saved us.*

Summer set down the persimmon and gave up the pretense of having tea.

"What do you want?" she asked.

"You must go into Meng's quarters and take his talisman stone. It is the source of all his power, which I must have if I am to defeat him and save you." Lady Wu offered her a small sketch of an ordinary-looking rock. "He will have concealed it, but I think with your power you will have no trouble finding it. It will likely be the only thing in the room that does not glitter."

The stone in the sketch matched the one Devalan had conjured for them back in Boston. Meng's talisman stone was TerraCairn.

The other woman took the sketch from Summer's hand and touched a corner of it to a lamp flame. She dropped it in an empty bowl and watched it burn.

"I do place great trust in you, Emissary's Wife,

but I know you will not disappoint me again. Not when you take such joy in bedding your husbands. To lose intimacy with them would be as painful as death, I think."

"Why would I lose it?"

Lady Wu made an elegant gesture with her hands. "If you fail me, I will have your husbands castrated."

• • • • •

Jadine Cutter sheathed her blades as she left her listening post outside the tea chamber and headed for the cool pantry. When the hall on either side of the storage door was clear Jadine slipped inside. She removed the dragon mask that concealed her scarred face.

"I know where it is," she said.

A short, grinning imp of a man popped up out of a grain sack.

"Well, it's about bloody time," he said. He shook off the bits of rice caught in his spiky red hair and offered her a peach. "Eat it," he said and tossed it to her. "Can't have you fainting in battle, darling girl."

"I don't faint," Jadine said as she caught the fruit. She devoured it in a few bites. "I need a

diversion so I can get to the treasure before
Summer Lautner does."

"That is why you smuggled me in here,"
Tryston reminded her. "Are you wanting a small
diversion, a large one, or something along the
lines of palace-demolishing?"

Another dragon man came into the pantry and
shut the door. When he took off his mask
Floronius's swarthy features dripped with sweat.

"They took the Lautner woman to Wu's tea
room," he said. "I think she means to kill her so
she can have her mates."

Jadine gave their dim-witted comrade a swat on
the back of the head.

"She's using her to get TerraCairn," Jadine said.
"Then she'll kill them all. It doesn't matter
anyway. I heard Lady Wu tell the Lautner bitch
where Meng is keeping the treasure. We'll get it
before she can, and go onto Chicago to get
ThunderBlade."

Floronius rubbed his scalp. "Can't we kill them
before we do?"

"Have you a brain beneath that thick skull?"
Tryston said and kicked his shin. "The master told
you that he wants them alive, you dolt."

Floronius didn't take offense, but leaned back
against the door and stared at the ceiling.

"I remember his orders and I carry them out," he said, then he looked down at Tryston. "Do you think he will be angry that we changed time back in Pompeii?"

"RainLance did that," Jadine said. "Besides, when we bring him all the crystals he'll be too happy to care." She pushed him aside to look out into the hall. "We're clear now. I'll go and collect the treasure. Tryston, you're with me. Work your magic, but don't bring the place down on our heads. Floronius, retrieve the portal and rendezvous with us in Xishan's throne room. Don't dally. Once Lady Wu knows the treasure is gone she'll go mad."

"What if I run into the Wiccans on the way?" Floronius demanded. "We can't kill them."

"True," Jadine said as she pulled the dragon mask back over her face. "But you can hurt them as much as you like."

• • • • •

Since Shelton had kissed her and then rejected her, Elettra felt as if any wrong move might set him off, so she kept away from him. Passing the time by idly extracting bits of crystal from the stone floor and massing it into a shimmering ball soon bored her. When a muffled, strange noise came from the outside hall Elettra went to the door and listened.

"I think the guards have left," she said. She ducked down to look through the gap under the door.

Shelton came to stand over her. "What is that racket?"

To Elettra's ears it sounded like distant rain. "Perhaps the first of the earthquakes to come."

She straightened and cupped the crystal mass between her hands, using her ability to compact and elongate it until it formed a thin, gleaming blade.

"The place is not shaking," the Templar told her as she slipped the blade into the door seam and lifted the outside latch. "They will attack us as soon as we are seen."

Elettra replaced the blade in her robe and shifted from her mortal guise into that of Lady Wu.

"I think not," she said and pressed a hand to his chest. His robe altered into the uniform of a dragon man.

"Very clever," the Templar said and covered her hand with his. "Will you forgive me for molesting you as I did?"

"To molest me you would have had to violate me in some fashion, but I did not mind it. 'Twas a strange delight."

Shelton's dark eyes glittered with heat. Though he looked as though he might say something, he didn't.

Elettra prodded the elaborate bundles of her now-black hair. "This is very uncomfortable. That woman should shave her head. Now come, we must be quick."

Shelton followed her out into the hall, which was deserted, and turned to face the noise that was growing louder and closer.

"Track the treasure. I will have your back."

The Templar seemed fond of her back, Elettra thought as she opened her senses, and picked up a trace of TerraCairn's immense power.

"This way," she said.

Once she had tracked TerraCairn to a room flanked by two heavily-armed guards Elettra reached for Shelton.

"Carry me," she told him. "I am not supposed to walk."

Shelton hoisted her into the cradle of his strong arms and paused. Their faces were so close their noses nearly touched.

"I have imagined how it would be to embrace

you," he said, holding her a little closer. "But I must confess that I never pictured it like this."

Elettra wanted to throw her arms around his neck, but forced herself to glower. "You are meant to be celibate."

"And you should still be buried in a diamond tomb," Shelton said and met her gaze.

"I should not have told you about my tomb," she said, exasperated. She did not understand him. Would he draw her close only to push her away again? "Carry me to that room. We must find the crystal and then Summer."

When Shelton carried Elettra up to the door, neither of the dragon men moved. Even so, she could see them staring at her through their mask's eye holes.

"The amazing Xishan commands you to admit me," Elettra said, and when the guards still didn't move she looked up at Shelton. "Put me down."

When he did she shifted into her true form, and rammed her fists into the guards' masks. Both men sagged to the floor as she took the keys from one and unlocked the chamber. Shelton helped her drag the men inside, and then straightened to gaze about in visible wonder.

"I think you have set yourself an impossible task," he said.

Elettra surveyed the treasure-filled room, which had been stuffed with urns overflowing with precious gems, coins, and jewels. Long strands of pale pearls hung in heavy curtains over trays heaped with gold and silver objects, and fat bundles of heavily-embroidered silks rose in shimmering stacks from open trunks. She couldn't sense where the treasure had been hidden, but then she saw a tall rack of diamond necklaces, bracelets and earbobs. The large quantity of the gems had to be blocking her from locating TerraCairn.

"It will take some time," Elettra said and spied a palm-sized clear sphere that had been inlaid with tiny fire gems. "It seems Kember did bring some Fae crystal here." She lifted the sculpture and turned it, making the gems flare with heat and light. "My sire kept a wall of these in his bath. He liked their glow."

Shelton touched her shoulder. "I will stand guard outside while you search."

She nodded and put down the sphere to begin the task of sorting through all the mortal treasures. Inside a hinged box of carved jade she found a pile of small, flat stone blocks that were plain on one side and etched on the other. The hinged sections of the box opened out until it formed a larger tray with recesses that resembled the courts and buildings of the palace. Elettra realized the flat blocks fit into the tray like puzzle pieces, which seemed more interesting to her than any of the mortal treasures. She knew it had taken great skill to carve the blocks so they fit together so perfectly.

But as she studied it more closely, her heart sank. She had been fooled.

The strange sound from the hall grew very loud, and then she heard Shelton shout. She folded the puzzle box back together, shoved it in her jacket, and rushed to the door.

"What is it?" she said. Something small and furry leapt onto her skirt and frantically climbed up the folds. "How does one rat make so much noise?"

"When it brings a million friends with it," Shelton said.

A shrieking, towering heap of the rodents flooded into the hall. The Templar pushed her back into the room, but they were both quickly engulfed by thousands of churning, scratching creatures. Elettra retreated backwards, brushing the rats from her face and head as their sharp claws raked her skin. They filled the room, piling atop each other as they climbed the ropes of

pearls toward the ceiling, and covered the trays
and trunks with their masses. The sound of wood
creaking and then splitting was the only warning
they had before the heavy rack of diamond
jewelry fell over. Thousands of tiny squeals filled
the air.

"We have to get out," Elettra yelled, but the
diamonds barred her way.

Shelton swept her up in his arms, leaped on top
of the rack of diamonds, and jumped through the
door. He ignored the river of small creatures as
he dashed back to their room. He shouldered the
door open, set her on the floor, and slammed the
door shut. Elettra dropped her mortal guise with
a heaving sigh of relief, as a few straggling rats
scurried under the bed.

"Are you all right?" Shelton asked. Something
clunked against her hip and she drew the puzzle
box from her pocket. "What is that?" he asked.
She handed it to him and he frowned. "Surely not
the treasure we seek?"

"No," she said. "It's only a toy puzzle." He
opened the box and emptied the pieces onto the
sheets, tossing the box beside it. "But it deceived
me."

He cocked his head at the objects. "This isn't a
toy or a puzzle," he said, scowling. Carefully he

began fitting the pieces into the frame, but turned them so their etched sides showed. "It's a map disguised as a tangram."

As Elettra peered more closely she saw that each stone piece had been carefully etched to show the different rooms and courtyards, which all had tiny, inlaid gems. Elettra quickly found the treasure room where they'd just been. Its piece was solidly paved with gems. The Room of Soft Sighs had been inlaid with lines to represent the hidden chamber and a tiny jade carved like an eye.

"This is a map of secrets," Elettra told Shelton. She pointed to a hidden room with lines etched around a tiny fleck of Fae crystal. "Here. This is Fae crystal, which explains why I sensed something in the treasure room. Find this room marked with the crystal, and we will find TerraCairn."

The door behind them opened and a guard strode into their chamber. As Shelton pushed her behind him, the guard pulled off his mask.

"Shelton," Bowers said, "we have to go." He looked at them both. "Now."

CHAPTER NINE

SUMMER COULDN'T BELIEVE it when
Elettra and Shelton walked in with Bowers
dressed like a guard. She'd just returned to Troy
and Michael and found their room unguarded.

"Where have you been?" she asked the
Templar.

"I followed Meng when he left the house
before dawn," Bowers said. "When I returned you
had already been arrested. I thought our host
might be in league with Wickerman, so I decided
to sneak into the palace."

Michael stepped closer, his expression cold.
"And how did you infiltrate the palace so easily?"

Bowers grinned. "I bribed the gate guards to
tell me where to find the shop of the tailor who
makes the palace guards' uniforms. I waited until
he closed up for the day, and broke in through the

roof. Once I had dressed the part I walked the moat and scouted the outer gates until I found the one the guards use. No one stopped me." He took out a bottle filled with a glittering liquid. "I found this in Meng's quarters. He's been making some kind of potion out of crystal, to give him power, or immortality, or both."

As Bowers handed the small vial to Michael, Shelton took out a puzzle box and assembled it into a map of the palace.

"Show us Meng's quarters," Shelton said to him.

"You don't believe me?" Bowers asked, his eyebrows arching.

"We would be happy to," Michael said, but gave the shorter Templar a narrow look. "Show us that your story is true."

"If I wanted you dead, Wiccan, I would have left you to rot in your silken prison." He jabbed his finger at the puzzle. "Meng's quarters are right there, in the Hall of Military Eminence." He looked at each of them. "Now have I proven my loyalty?"

"If we find it there," Troy said.

"We waste time," Elettra said.

"She's right," Summer said slowly. She didn't entirely believe the Templar's story, but they would have to sort it out later. "We need to go to Meng's quarters now," she said to Bowers. "Will you guide us there?"

He put on his mask and led them through the rat littered halls, across the main plaza, and into the Hall of Military Eminence. Although platoons of soldiers moved through the compound, none of them paid attention to Summer or her group. She suspected that Lady Wu had played a part in freeing them from captivity and attention, so that they could do her bidding.

They skirted the throne room where their sentence had been passed, and Summer couldn't help but stare at the place they'd stood. But Bowers quickly led them past it to a short corridor. Again Summer noted that there were no guards to stop them, until they arrived in an antechamber with doors branching off in different directions—and a corpse. Rats swarmed over the body of the guard, who had been killed with a single sword-thrust to the heart.

"It's the same wound we saw on the women at the seaside brothel," Troy said as he inspected the wound. "Wickerman's people are inside the palace."

"Here it is," Bowers said, motioning to one of the doors.

Meng's chamber occupied a suite of rooms in the inner court. When Summer stepped inside the front room she could feel traces of malevolent magic all around her.

"Don't touch anything," she warned them as she inspected the hundreds of crystal objects the magician had assembled and displayed. "Elettra?"

"This is why I did not sense its presence," the Fae woman said tightly. "Most of these crystals are flawed. The devices he fashioned from them cannot be used. TerraCairn intended to harm a great many mortals if he had."

Troy went still. "What do you mean, it intended?"

"All of the crystals are alive, in a fashion," the Fae woman said slowly. "They are not flesh like us, but they have minds. They can think, and dream, and plan. They were created to be weapons, and to kill, so the only true pleasure they can feel is by causing such things to happen. They will even use those like Meng to help them by deceiving them into believing they wish to serve. All they truly want is a chance to destroy anyone and anything."

Shelton looked sick. "And you never thought to say this before now?"

"I did not wish to frighten you," Elettra

admitted.

Summer smelled a foul odor and went to a tall vermillion wood cabinet behind Meng's desk.

"There's something dead in here," she said.

As soon as she lifted her hand to the panel it swung open, knocking her back from the hidden space behind it. A mangled corpse hung dangling from a hook, its ravaged face smiling at her with small, pearly teeth.

"A bit too late to have tea with Mr. Meng," said a short, red haired man as he and a dragon guard emerged from the adjoining room. "Let us leave in peace, brothers and sisters, or we'll have to get nasty."

"You terrify me," Troy said drily.

"Nasty it is, then," the cultist said, and snapped his fingers.

A brittle sound of stone grinding on stone came from another room, and the floor shook as a huge tiger emerged from the shadows. As it did the cultists hurried toward the door, only to have their paths blocked by Summer's mates and the Templars.

"You're not going anywhere," Troy assured them.

The dragon guard produced two lethal looking blades.

Summer forgot to breathe as she looked into the stone tiger's amber eyes, and felt the magic that animated it radiate like a sickness into the room. Impossibly, Elettra stepped toward it as the monstrous creation padded forward. Summer grabbed her arm and tried to haul her back.

Michael stepped into the big cat's path. "Here, kitty, kitty."

The stone tiger lifted its head and opened its jaws as if it were roaring, but the only sound that came from it was the grinding of rock. It swiped at Michael with a massive paw, shredding the front of his robe, and then crouched down as if to leap.

"Move," Elettra said, shoving Summer aside.

As the creature leaped, Elettra knocked Michael away and lifted her hands. Power enveloped the springing tiger, which crumbled into a pile of dust.

"I'm not so impressed with these stone cats," Shelton said grinning at her.

But the dragon guard rushed forward and kicked the crystal debris pile, sending dust everywhere. It landed in the faces of the four men guarding the door, and Summer felt it pelt her hair as she turned away. At the same time the little man with red hair motioned at the hallway behind them. The flood of rodents was immediate.

"Michael," Summer screamed, "look out!"

As the dragon guard lunged at him, he wiped his eyes, but Troy managed to shove him out of the way at the last second. But the big man bumped into the much smaller Bowers, creating an opening to the door. The dragon guard darted for it, but Elettra dove and tackled the cultist, landing them both in a swarm of rats.

But as they rolled, an ordinary stone fell out of the guard's jacket, coming to a stop at Summer's feet. As the edge of it brushed her toes, it began to glitter with a pale yellow light. Cracks in the stone floor beneath it shot out in all directions. The ground beneath the palace began to quake.

"TerraCairn!" Summer shouted over the din.

But before she could pick up the treasure the red-haired man scooped it up, shoving her aside. She flew backward landing hard on the floor, but saw the man give her a snide grin. As he raced away, more rats poured into the room. As the ground rocked beneath her, Summer couldn't get to her feet and was instantly covered in the tiny, frantic creatures. But just as quickly, two strong hands lifted her clear.

"Michael!" she gasped, pointing at the red head as he darted through the door. "He has TerraCairn."

All around them the room shuddered as crystal sculptures teetered on the shelves. Both the dragon guard and Elettra had regained their feet. As they squared off, it took the Fae woman blinding speed to avoid the cultist's blades.

As the vermillion cabinet rocked in place, Michael dragged Summer away from it. It crashed just behind them, as Elettra leapt toward a case of crystal sculptures, propping it up with both hands.

The dragon guard saw the opportunity, launching at Elettra's back. But Shelton and Bowers were already in motion. As Shelton grabbed Elettra, Bowers grabbed a chair and ran forward with it. The dragon guard ducked under the chair, spun with blades flashing, and dashed out the door.

Summer suddenly realized the quake had stopped, and that most of the rats had flowed back into the hallway, following the cultists.

"Michael," Troy yelled. "I'm going after them. You're with Summer."

But before he reached the door he halted and backed away.

Lady Wu hobbled inside, her expression more smug than ever as she surveyed the ruined room. Meng's corpse lay half-exposed under the cabinet.

"How often our kindnesses are returned with

savagery," she said.

"About as often as innocence is punished with treachery," Summer said, trembling with rage, as it all became clear. Dragon men began pouring into the room. "You wanted someone to take the blame. That's why you had us arrested, and kept here like guests. You needed to accuse us of your crimes."

"I am not standing beside the tortured remains of my husband's most trusted man," Lady Wu simpered. She turned to her guards. "It seems these strangers have murdered the court magician. Seize them."

As the guards grabbed them and dragged them from the room Summer wondered if she should try to transport them without forming a circle.

No, Daughter, the Emerald Tablet warned. *Only you would go forward in time.*

A powerful tremor rocked the walls, but the palace guard marched them on until they'd reached the throne room. Two eunuchs placed Lady Wu on the throne, while the dragon men circled Summer and her team, each with a pike aimed at them. Another violent jolt rocked the palace, as the columns of giant metal warriors shook.

Behind Lady Wu, the floor-to-ceiling silk screen

rippled. Summer looked up just in time to see it detach from the roof. As light as air, it drifted down, crumpling and sliding as it went, until it lay in a white heap behind the throne. But as the tableau it revealed came into view, Summer put a hand to her mouth.

There was the governor in his square hat—as a terra cotta statue. Placed on rollers, it stood just in front of a deeply curved silver mirror, at whose center was an unlit torch. Summer searched the ceiling panels and found what she expected: two eye-shaped holes in the ornate panels.

"Parrot," Michael murmured.

Her statue stood off to the side, her face worried as she touched the half-coin pendant on her chest. More statues of women filled the hidden chamber, too many to count.

"Since you have proven to be assassins instead of emissaries," Lady Wu said. "Your sentences will be carried out immediately." She nodded to her guards. "Death by slow slicing."

"Your husband didn't find tranquility five years ago," she said to Lady Wu. "You murdered him, and hid his bones in the statue. It's why you murdered all those women. You had to make it look like he was still alive, so you kept bringing concubines for him to the palace. You couldn't let any of them live because they would have told someone that they never saw your husband. You have been the governor all this time."

Lady Wu laughed. "Now that Meng is dead, I no longer have to share my throne with anyone." She took out a bottle of glittering liquid. "Or his immortality potion. I drink this, and I will rule forever."

A much more violent tremor made pieces of the roof crack and fall.

"This city is about to be destroyed," Troy shouted at the guards. "Leave us and get to open ground."

Lady Wu clapped her hands together as if she were delighted. "Such compassion for my men, when you had none for Meng."

"We didn't kill them," Summer said to the guard approaching her. "I swear it."

"I know," an amused feminine voice said as the guard used the tip of her sword to slash Summer's arm. "She did the husband, but I killed Meng. As soon as my partners show up we'll leave you to die with the rest of the city."

"What if they don't show up?" Summer said. "I'm the only one who can save you."

"My mother used to say that, before I cut off her head." She rested her blade between

Summer's breasts. "I can't decide what to slice off next."

Emerald light shot out of the wound on Summer's arm, knocking away the female guard and driving back the others from Summer's team. The verdant light coalesced in front of them, taking on the shape of an enormous glowing dragon. The great beast undulated around the room, stunning the guards with blasts of verdant power. As the guards retreated, another tremor rocked the room. Elettra, Shelton, and Bowers were barely able to stumble toward her.

Summer gasped as Lady Wu's throne fell over, trapping her underneath it.

The female guard scramble to her feet, and joined her short, red-haired partner as well as someone else she recognized.

"Floronius?" Summer breathed.

But no sooner had she uttered his name, than the glowing green dragon rose up behind him. It opened its giant jaws over his head and snapped them shut.

The cultist's body began to disintegrate into bits and then chunks of straw, collapsing to the shattered stone floor in a heap.

"One of Wickerman's golems," Troy said.

The small, red-haired man extended his arm

out, holding what looked like a round silver picture frame that filled with a starry blackness as it stretched itself wide.

"Form a circle," Summer shouted to her team, as another quake began.

The groan of tortured metal filled the room as the massive metal soldier beside her suddenly buckled. A crushing weight struck her on the head. Summer fell, her head spinning madly as the ground under her convulsed.

"Beauty?" Michael said as he snatched her up in his arms. *"Troy."*

Summer peered up at him as her vision grayed. "Oh, no."

Time seemed to slow as her thoughts unraveled. They had thought of everything for this quest, except what they would do if something happened to her. Only she had the power to move them through time. Only she could save them from the worst earthquake in human history.

Please, no.

Summer felt the warmth of her own blood streaking down her neck and shoulder, and saw the terrible fear in her lover's eyes.

"I love—"

Darkness came, and she fell into an abyss.

• • • • •

The End of *Palace of Pleasure*

• • • • •

Summer's story continues in *House of Desire (Book Fourteen of the Silver Wood Coven Series)*.

For a sneak peek, turn the page.

House of Desire (Book Fourteen of the Silver Wood Coven Series)
Excerpt

Summer opened her eyes to find herself in an enormous cavern. Millennia of dripping water and shifting earth had carved the space out of solid rock, but something more intelligent had built within it a magnificent cathedral of crystallized stone.

The light that illuminated it came from within the sparkling walls, as if some mystic energy had been trapped inside them. In the center of the cathedral lay a beautiful deep pool of turquoise water. From its center a solid column of silent, white-gold fire streamed from the surface to an enormous crystal dome set into the very peak of the cavern.

She lay still as she tried to remember what had happened. TerraCairn, the crystal of earth, had been dropped, and set off the Great Shaanxi Earthquake. Something had collapsed on her in the palace throne room. Her throat tightened as she recalled the horror she'd felt, looking up at

Michael and Troy while feeling herself slipping away. She'd known that by losing consciousness she'd condemned them to die along with the rest of their team. No one but Summer had the power to jump through time.

A splash of water on her cheek made her gasp and sit up. The sudden movement sent a shaft of intense pain through her head. She had to bite her lip to hold back a cry of pain. Carefully she reached up to touch the deep wound on her scalp.

I wouldn't do that, a cold, flat voice said inside her mind. *It will burn.*

Summer turned around to see a water sprite standing behind her. Unlike those she had encountered in Pompeii and the bay of Naples, this one was much larger. It had to be twice her height, and its bulk seethed like a huge wave preparing to crash. The liquid that gave it form had a murkiness like the sky filled with storm clouds. It had a vaguely humanoid shape, but no features or gender. Everything about the creature made Summer's skin crawl, but she kept her revulsion from showing on her face.

"What are you?" she asked.

You know me, it said. Now the voice sounded sharp, like ice cracking. *I came to you in amity, and you cast me out.*

Summer pressed her fingertips to the wound, and the blood from it seared her skin like a red-hot iron. She snatched her hand away to see blisters bubbling on her fingers.

I did warn you, the water sprite said. Its blank face shimmered as it sank down into a puddle beside her, keeping only its upper torso intact. *Why will you not open to me?*

Suddenly Summer recognized the voice. "You're RainLance."

Thus they said when they took me from my sepulcher. The sprite used the end of one watery appendage to draw a curve across the lower half of its face. *Do you wish to know my true name, fair one? I will give you all my secrets. Only drink of me. Let me fill you, and you shall become our Queen.*

"No," Summer said. "Get away from me."

She rose and staggered away from the sprite, only to stop short when a giant stone tiger appeared in her path. It limped toward her, a colossal version of the animated cats they had encountered in Huaxian. Amber light spilled from its broken paw, and she felt her own wound throb so painfully she nearly collapsed.

Little sack of meat, the tiger said as it paced around her. Its movements created a horrific grinding sound from its stone joints. *I shall tear your entrails from your belly and adorn myself with them. Then I will have the last of the GemSlaves. We shall devour her slowly, one bite at a time, while the simpleton screams.*

"Her name is GemSage," Summer said, "and she is not stupid." The cold of the creature chilled her shaking hand, but she willed herself to remain perfectly still. "As for me, I never touched you."

Liar.

An image appeared on the surface of the cave lake, showing the stone rolling across the floor of Meng's quarters and stopping at Summer's toes. Now she could see the small crack that appeared where her flesh had touched the rock.

Was it possible that she could injure the crystals?

"I'm sorry that you were hurt," she said.

The tiger lifted its massive head and opened its jaws as if to roar. No sound came from its throat, but the cavern began to shake. As stones dropped all around Summer hobbled to a recess in the wall. She watched as part of the cathedral collapsed in a sparkling cloud of rubble.

Let me have her, said a different voice. A cold wind blasted her, rushing away to whirl through the debris. It gathered the crumbled stone and crystal and swirled it into a monstrous tornado that turned and roared across the cavern toward Summer. *I want to hear her squeak as I squeeze the last breath of life from her.*

Why should she be yours? a new voice said. A tiny imp made of flame appeared in front of the whirlwind. It flared up into an immense, crackling bonfire. The flames shaped themselves into an arc that spun toward Summer. *I need to feed.*

The water sprite swelled over her. *Give yourself to us, fair one, or we will take you.*

Summer knew that the rogues had RainLance and TerraCairn, while ThunderBlade, the crystal of air, and SunCask, the crystal of Fire, still remained lost in time. That meant none of this could be happening in the real world.

"You'll do nothing to me," Summer said. Feeling more confident now, she pushed herself away from the wall. "This is just a dream."

Is it? all four said.

MORE BOOKS BY HAZEL HUNTER

SILVER WOOD COVEN SERIES

Though she's taken the name given her by a kind stranger, Summer can no more explain waking up homeless and covered in blood, than she can the extreme attraction drawing people to her. Amnesiac, confused, and frightened, she's not even aware that she's a witch. But help arrives in two very different forms: the cool and restrained Templar Michael Charbon and his centuries-long friend Wiccan Major Troy Atwater.

Rescued (Silver Wood Coven Book One)

Stolen (Silver Wood Coven Book Two)

United (Silver Wood Coven Book Three)

Betrayed (Silver Wood Coven Book Four)

Revealed (Silver Wood Coven Book Five)

Silver Wood Coven Box Set (Books 1 - 5)

Lost (Silver Wood Coven Book Six)

Divided (Silver Wood Coven Book Seven)

Gone (Silver Wood Coven Book Eight)

Burned (Silver Wood Coven Book Nine)

Reclaimed (Silver Wood Coven Book Ten)

Call of Fate (Silver Wood Coven Book Eleven)

Sea of Love (Silver Wood Coven Book Twelve)

Palace of Pleasure (Silver Wood Coven Book Thirteen)

House of Desire (Silver Wood Coven Book

Fourteen)

Sign up for my newsletter to be notified of new releases!

THE FOREVER FAIRE SERIES

She's found a magical lover. But is he real?
Kayla Rowe and her little sister are running for their lives. Chased from town to town by a gang of bikers that no one else sees, Kayla is down to her last dollar and out of ideas. But when she stumbles into the winter camp of a man who is larger than life, her world changes.

Hunted (Forever Faire Book One)

Outcast (Forever Faire Book Two)

Hidden (Forever Faire Book Three)

Denied (Forever Faire Book Four)

Destined (Forever Faire Book Five)

Forever Faire Box Set (Books 1 - 5)

THE SANCTUARY COVEN SERIES

An innocent, young woman. A single-minded

warlock. A web of seduction that ensnares them

both. Life is finally starting to work out for

Heather Moore: a place all her own, a fulfilling

career, and a wonderful new man in her life.

Straight from the pages of a magazine, her

French lover is the stuff of dreams. Strong and

sexy, considerate and funny, it's as though she's

been waiting from him all her short life.

Twice Seduced (Sanctuary Coven Book One)

Taken Together (Sanctuary Coven Book Two)

Matched Mates (Sanctuary Coven Book Three)

Primal Partners (Sanctuary Coven Book Four)

Forever Joined (Sanctuary Coven Book Five)

Sanctuary Coven Box Set (Books 1 - 5)

THE HOLLOW CITY COVEN SERIES

A daring quest. A deadly enemy. A protector
who won't quit. Although Wiccan Gillian
Granger's life's work is finding a legendary city,
her research in musty libraries hasn't prepared
her for the field, let alone a gorgeous escort.

Shayne Savatier knows he's on a milk run,

especially after he meets his beautiful charge.

But when enemies attack her, everything

changes. Passion intertwines with protection,

and duty bonds hard with desire.

Possessed (Hollow City Coven Book One)

Shadowed (Hollow City Coven Book Two)

Trapped (Hollow City Coven Book Three)

Haunted (Hollow City Coven Book Four)

Remembered (Hollow City Coven Book Five)

Reborn (Hollow City Coven Book Six)

Hollow City Coven Box Set (Books 1 - 6)

THE CASTLE COVEN SERIES

Novice witch Hailey Devereaux had resolved to live life as an outsider. Possessed of a unique Wiccan ability, her own people shun her. But that all ends when two very different men enter her life: the brooding Major Kieran McCallen and Coven Master Piers Dayton. But their training and tests are only the beginning. As she struggles to fulfill her destiny and find her place in the world, Hailey also discovers love.

Found (Castle Coven Book One)

Abandoned (Castle Coven Book Two)

Healed (Castle Coven Book Three)

Claimed (Castle Coven Book Four)

Imprisoned (Castle Coven Book Five)

Sacrificed (Castle Coven Book Six)

Castle Coven Box Set (Books 1 - 6)

THE MAGUS CORPS SERIES

Meet the warlocks of the Magus Corps, sworn to protect Wiccans at all costs. As they find and track fledgling witches, it's a race against an ancient enemy that would rather see all Wiccans dead. But where danger and intimacy come together, passion is never far behind.

Dominic (Her Warlock Protector Book 1)

Sebastian (Her Warlock Protector Book 2)

Logan (Her Warlock Protector Book 3)

Colin (Her Warlock Protector Book 4)

Vincent (Her Warlock Protector Book 5)

Jackson (Her Warlock Protector Book 6)

Trent (Her Warlock Protector Book 7)

Her Warlock Protector Box Set (Books 1 - 7)

THE SECOND SIGHT SERIES

Join psychic Isabelle de Grey and FBI profiler Mac MacMillan as they hunt a serial killer in the streets of Los Angeles. Even as their search closes in on the kidnapper, they discover not only clues, but a fiery passion that quickly consumes them.

Touched (Second Sight Book 1)

Torn (Second Sight Book 2)

Taken (Second Sight Book 3)

Chosen (Second Sight Book 4)

Charmed (Second Sight Book 5)

Changed (Second Sight Book 6)

Second Sight Box Set (Books 1 - 6)

THE PASSAGE TO PASSION SERIES

Travel the world in these breathless tales of

erotic romance. Each features a different couple

in fast-paced tales of fiery passion.

Arctic Exposure

In an Alaskan storm, a young couple cling to

each for life and for love.

Desert Thirst

In the Sahara, a master tracker has the scent of

his fiery client.

Jungle Fever

A forensic accountant blossoms under the care

of a plantation owner in Thailand.

Mountain Wilds

A beautiful doctor on the rebound crashes with

her pilot in British Columbia.

Island Magic

Two treasure-hunting scuba divers are

kidnapped in the Caribbean.

Passage to Passion - The Complete Collection

This box set includes all five books: Arctic Exposure, Desert Thirst, Jungle Fever, Mountain Wilds, and Island Magic.

THE ROMANCE IN THE RUINS NOVELS

Explore the ancient world and the new in these standalone novels of erotic romance. Each features a hero and heroine who come together against all odds, in exotic and remote settings where danger and love are found in equal measure.

Words of Love

Set in the heartland of the ancient Maya.

Labyrinth of Love

Set on the ancient Greek island of Crete.

Stars of Love

Set in the rugged Pueblo Southwest.

Sign up for my newsletter to be notified of new

releases!

ENJOY THIS BOOK?

You can make a big difference.

Reviews are the most powerful tools in my arsenal when it comes to getting attention for my books. Much as I'd like to, I don't have the financial muscle of a New York publisher. I can't take out full pages ads in the newspaper or put posters on the subway.

(Not yet, anyway.)

But I do have something much more powerful and effective than that, and it's something that those publishers would kill to get their hands on.

A committed and loyal group of readers.

Honest reviews of my books help bring them to the attention of other readers.

If you've enjoyed this book I would be very grateful if you could spend just five minutes leaving a review   it can be as short as you like.

Thank you so much!

DEDICATION

For Mr. H.

Made in the USA
Coppell, TX
17 June 2020

28183155R10089